TIME'S FOOL
AND OTHER STORIES

by
Grant Carrington

TIME'S FOOL
AND OTHER STORIES

Brief Candle
Press

Publishing History: *Time's Fool*, Doubleday 1981; *Time's Fool and Other Stories*, Variations on a Theme 2013

Cover Design by Rob Kroese

First Brief Candle Press edition published 2015
www.briefcandlepress.com

ISBN: 978-1-942319-14-6

DEDICATION:

This one's for my mother

CONTENTS

But thought's the slave of life, and time, time's fool;
And time, that takes survey of all the world,
Must have a stop.

King Henry IV, Part I
William Shakespeare
Act V, Scene 4

Time's Fool...

The city was now clearly visible all around them, a panoramic view. All the strings of light seemed to converge on this building, like spokes in a wheel, although Garcia knew it was only an illusion, like the illusion that the Earth was the center of the universe. Across the spokes, other rays of light crossed and recrossed, moving out in waves of light from the building to the distant horizon, until they disappeared in the distance. The jewels of the city glowed and glittered all around them. The wind blew viciously across the top of the building, carrying traces of smoke and remnants of odd perfumes, intermingled smells of distant factories and nearby buildings.

If his heart was pounding now, it was not in fear but in exultation. He was alive, come what may, come death and extinction, as surely it must. You can't go back, he thought, and you can't stand still. He had to go forward or he would surely die. That was where his strength, and his art lay, in the constant fight against Death, spitting in its very face, not in conquering it and then living in a fearful immortality. So he would die. So what? In the meantime, he would live life to its fullest, not cringing before time...

ANNAPOLIS TOWN

When most people think of Annapolis, they think of the Naval Academy. They don't think of it as the capital of Maryland, with the State House and legislative offices.

To me, Annapolis is like an old New England town, with its narrow streets, the gentle hills leading down to Chesapeake Bay, the cobblestoned area around City Dock, where a dimestore faces out onto the Severn River, and with its two old traffic circles and the two-century-old campus of St. John's College.

It reminds me of the shoreline towns of my native Rhode Island. I guess that's why I moved here as soon as I discovered it. It's an hour's drive each way to my job with the federal government in Washington, but it's worth the extra trouble.

For one thing, there's Tom Raymond's guitar shop. Tom is one of the best independent guitar makers left in the country. Most of his time is spent in repairing instruments but he manages to turn out about ten guitars a year, each unique, each different, each very simple, and every one of them well made. The few times he makes a mistake, he scraps it and starts all over.

I was hanging around in his shop on a Saturday afternoon, the salt wind blowing from the bay up the narrow alley to his shop, when she walked in. She stopped at in the doorway, smelling the sawdust in the air and blinking to adjust her eyes from the bright spring sun. The sunlight, sectored by the old windowpane, seemed to glow on her pale yellow shift.

She saw me standing there talking to Tom, who was busy sandpapering the shellac off someone's fiddle, and immediately disregarded me.

"Are you Tom Raymond?" she asked Tom.

Tom grunted a reply. Sometimes I think he has some New Englander in him.

"You make guitars?"

"Yep."

"I'd like you to make a guitar for me."

"You would." It was an uninflected statement, not a question.

"I have the drawings here."

I walked over to look at the papers she was spreading out on one of the benches. They were neatly drawn, with braces, dimensions, and cross-views all clearly indicated.

"Who drew these?" Tom asked, a note of interest creeping into his voice.

"I did."

"Are you a draftsman?"

"Not exactly. I took the measurements from a guitar I once owned. It was destroyed in a silly accident."

He pointed to a place on the drawing. "You don't want a brace here. That would be unnecessary."

"I think that would result in some interesting harmonics," she said.

For fifteen minutes they discussed the drawings, the deficiencies of the design, improvements that could be made, and the woods to be used for the sides, top, bottom, and neck.

"Eight strings," Tom said. "You sure you want eight strings, ma'am?"

"Yes. What's wrong with that?"

"Well, most guitars have six or twelve strings."

"Oh..." She said it as if she didn't know.

"Of course," I said, "there are plenty of oddly-strung guitars. Big Joe Williams uses nine strings and Spider John Koerner has a seven-string National, doesn't he, Tom?"

He nodded. "I guess you'd have to use an open tuning with this thing."

"What?" The confidence she had when she entered the shop was rapidly disappearing.

"An open tuning," he repeated, but didn't explain. "What are you going to use for the extra strings?"

"Oh, I'll have special ones made."

Tom snorted.

"Will you do it?"

"I suppose so. It'll cost you around five hundred dollars, though."

"Money is no problem," she said eagerly. "How soon can you have it done?"

"Well, I've got a lot of work to do before I can get to it. I'll have to order some of the woods. It'll be a couple of months at least, but I should be able to get it done within half a year if I don't run into any trouble."

"But I must have it sooner. I'll pay you double, one thousand dollars, if you do it immediately."

Tom gathered the papers together and handed them to her. "Lady, there are people who are depending on me to do work for them first. You're no better than they are."

They don't make many like Tom any more.

She stood there, not yet accepting the drawings. "Two months?" she whispered, nearly pleading.

"I can try. No promises. But I'll try."

❧ ◄ ► ❧

I didn't see her again until the next Wednesday. Each Wednesday evening some of the local musicians get together in Tom's shop to play bluegrass. Apparently she had seen the little card in a corner of a window that mentions the get-together.

She listened to them play, sing, and joke for about fifteen minutes then she walked back out into the street.

I followed her. She was standing in the alley, looking at the children who raced up and down the narrow street and watching the people loafing on their porches, listening to the music that drifted out of the shop.

"Kind of peaceful out here like this," I said. She looked up and apparently recognized me. "Like something out of the past."

Her head jerked around suddenly. "What do you mean?"

"Well, it's sort of like a scene out of the Nineteenth Century, if you can ignore the automobiles." I nodded toward the old people, dressed in their old-style clothes, long dresses, and pants held up by suspenders. My white shirt and casual pants were more in keeping with the scene than her miniskirt.

She smiled. "Yes, I guess it is." Then she made a grimace and gestured toward the shop. "Is that the only kind of... music they know how to make?"

"They're bluegrass musicians. It's still popular music around here."

She shook her head. "What about you? You were here the other day. What's your connection with this?"

"Nothing much. I just like music, and Tom's an interesting person to talk with."

"You don't play an instrument?"

"I fool around with the guitar a little."

"Why aren't you in there?"

"I play classical guitar."

"Really? I'd like to hear you some time. I think I'd enjoy that more than this bluegrass."

"Well," I said, "my apartment's a couple of blocks over."

She laughed delightedly. "Ah, you're going to try to seduce me."

But as we walked over, she slipped her hand inside my arm, and we walked through the picturesque streets of Annapolis town like a Nineteenth Century couple... in miniskirt and tapered trousers.

$\otimes \blacktriangleleft \blacktriangleright \infty$

From the outside, the building where I have my apartment looks rather shabby. It's just another dwelling shoehorned into a line of row houses that marches up one of the Annapolis hills.

But inside, on the second floor, I have a nice little nest. It isn't big, barely more than a large efficiency, but an excellent stereo, several posters, expensive throw rugs, and good furniture have turned it into a home.

I turned on the low-level amber light, poured a couple of glasses of Mateus, and took my Goya out of its case. It didn't faze her, so I knew there was no sense in wasting anything difficult on her, and I played a few short pieces I had composed when I was younger, nothing fancy.

"Radcliffe," she said delightedly.

"I beg your pardon?"

"Radcliffe. Didn't he compose that music?"

"Yes. Yes, he did," I said emphasizing the word *he*. "But how did *you* know?"

"Well, I... I..." she stuttered, suddenly all flustered again. "I must have heard it somewhere."

"Yes, I would imagine so. But where? I'd like to know."

"Well, why? What's so important about it?" Her laugh was nervous.

"Because *I* wrote it. I'm Dick Radcliffe."

She looked at me, her mouth slightly open, a strange trapped look in her eyes. "You're Richard Radcliffe."

I nodded.

"Oh, that's marvelous."

"I'm glad you think so. I'm not so sure I agree with you. Are you sure you don't know where you heard them?"

"Oh, I'd love to tell you if I could. But I can't. I honestly can't, Mr. Radcliffe."

"I wish you'd call me Dick."

"Oh. I'm sorry. My name is Nikki. Nikki Wenz."

"I know," I said. "You gave Tom your name when you ordered your guitar last Saturday."

"Oh." She looked around, perhaps beginning to feel trapped with a strange man in his apartment. She stared at the kitchenette, the drapes, the furniture.

"Would you like to go?" I asked.

"Where?"

"I mean, if you feel nervous here..."

"Oh, no. It's very interesting, being in a bachelor's apartment. Especially that of a famous composer."

"I'm not a famous composer."

"But you will be. I know it. You'll see." She had her smug assurance back.

"Glad to hear it." I started to tune the guitar back to standard.

"You're composing now, aren't you?"

"No, I've given that up. I work for the government."

"But you mustn't give it up, Dick. You're too good for that."

I sighed. "No, it's too tough a life for me, Nikki. I thought of becoming a concert guitarist once, but I'm just not that ambitious. So I got a degree in computer science instead."

She was silent for a while. "Maybe it's just as well. Maybe you have to live a while longer, mature a bit. But don't give up composing for good, Dick; you've got too much talent."

If there ever was a conversation-stopper, that was it. We both sat there, not knowing what to say, both, I guess, a little embarrassed.

She held up her glass. "This is very good. Could I have some more please?"

I refilled her glass and sat down again on the bed, facing her and examining her as she continued to examine my apartment. She wasn't particularly good-looking, but she had good legs, small exquisite breasts, and the most fantastically perfect skin. And there was an ingenuous air about her that wasn't broken even by her strange moments of bewilderment and suspicion. She had a natural grace that made me feel she would be at ease if she were stark naked in front of Congress.

"Don't you have a woman?" she asked suddenly.

"No. Not at the moment."

"Why?"

"I don't know." I busied myself with putting the Goya back in its case while I thought. "Most of the girls I grew up with are married, and so are the people I work with. I have no way of meeting single girls. So I just sort of stumble into them, like I did with you."

"Don't worry," she said. "You'll meet the love of your life soon. I know it."

I grinned. "Maybe I already have."

She looked at me blankly for a moment before the meaning sank in. Then she smiled very faintly. "No, I'm afraid not. But thank you for the thought, Dick."

I wasn't about to let her get off that easily. "Is there someone else?"

"No, not exactly."

"Then can I see you every now and then until I meet the... love of my life?"

She didn't even blush. I don't think she realized I was making fun of her. She just sat there, pensive. "I could use a ride into Washington, if you ever go there," she said at last.

"I work there."

"Then why do you live here? Washington is so far away."

"Not all that far. And I like Annapolis. It's so filled with the past." She nodded. "It gives me a sense of continuity with the past."

She looked at me as though I knew something I shouldn't. "What do you mean?" she asked sharply.

"Well, like when we were back at Tom's. I can see people dressed as they were a hundred years ago, almost as though nothing had changed."

She sat back in the chair. "Yes, Annapolis does have an air of timelessness." She smiled. "Almost as if it will be here forever."

"The way it is now."

She shook her head. "But some day there will be archaeologists puzzling over its ruins as they do over... what's that city?"

"Pompeii?"

"Is that where they fought the war over a girl?"

"No. Troy, Helen of Troy."

"Yes. That's the one."

There was another moment of petered-out conversation before I asked, "What do you want to go to Washington for?"

"Oh, I'm a historian. I've got a lot of research to do. That's why I'm here."

"You're an historian, and you forgot Helen of Troy?"

She got a little flustered again. "Well, my specialty is American history. It's been so long since I studied ancient history and it all got pushed out by new facts."

That didn't ring quite true to me. After all, I'm not a historian at all, but I know the story of Helen of Troy. Everyone does.

"You see, that's why we can't get too serious about each other. I'll be leaving in a couple of months."

"When?"

"Whenever I finish my research. There's so much I can do in Washington. That would be wonderful, Dick. Would you mind?"

Would I mind? Would I mind if my pay were doubled? Would I mind if Segovia were to take me on as a pupil?

ঙ◄►ঙ

I picked her up the next morning at the state legislature parking lot. She was wearing another minidress and carrying a small camera.

On the way to Washington on Route 50, a throughway, she told me how she planned to just walk around Washington at first, getting the feel of it.

I suggested places she could go: the Smithsonian buildings, Georgetown, the Phillips Gallery, Dupont Circle.

And we made plans to meet for lunch.

I felt embarrassed for some reason when I pulled into the parking lot I'd been using for two years, but the attendant acted as though I drove in with an attractive woman every day.

We walked to my office building. As I was saying goodbye to her, reminding her to meet me for lunch, she stretched up on her toes and kissed me lightly.

"Goodbye," she said, and was gone in the crowd of office workers hurrying to get to their desks.

I floated through the morning but I came down hard when she wasn't waiting for me at lunchtime. All kinds of thoughts flitted through my head and they all dwelled on the possible meanings of that "goodbye."

But she hurried up ten minutes later, all breathless and eager to tell me about her morning explorations. She told me how she had walked to Georgetown and gotten engrossed in the hippie shops, the sandal shop, the record stores.

"It's so picturesque," she said breathlessly.

I took her to a small restaurant on Connecticut Avenue and, because we were so late, we had a hard time getting served. But that meant that much more time I could spend with her.

We parted as before, with a quick kiss and a promise to meet outside my office building at five.

We spent the evening walking the streets of Annapolis, looking at the boats, buying a bottle of red wine, and going to my apartment to listen to records, and to communicate.

Our communication didn't require many words.

The pattern was repeated the next day and, during the weekend, we drove around Maryland and Virginia, visiting Great Falls and Skyline Drive.

Sometime during the next week, she moved in with me.

She had remarkably few clothes for a woman. She was able to carry them all in a small brand-new suitcase. She had two dresses, two skirts, a few tops, and lots of diaphanous underthings. She was the only woman I've known who bought those things for herself, although I'd bought them for my girlfriends in the past.

The next few months were filled with explorations of Maryland and Virginia that I'd never gone on by myself, from Fort Washington and Mount Vernon to the strip joints of The Block in Baltimore. We even took a weekend trip to New York City.

We spent a couple of afternoons looking for a machine shop to draw and wrap the wire for her strings. We finally found one in Anacostia. It was going to be expensive.

It was all wonderful, and the most wonderful moments of all were the simple ones, like the time we fed squirrels in Lafayette Park across from the White House.

Nikki burst into the apartment, her face alive with excitement. "It's finished, Dick, it's finished!"

"What's finished?" I asked as she whirled across the room and collapsed in the chair in a tangle of pretty legs and sexy lingerie.

"The guitar. Tom's finished the guitar."

I'd completely forgotten about it in the months we'd been together. I hard hardly been to Tom's at all, but now I began to suspect that some of the times when she'd gone out alone, she'd gone to Tom's. It wasn't jealousy, mind you; I knew Nikki was interested in no one but me.

"We'll have to pick up the strings tomorrow," she said.

"Okay." I grinned. "I'm curious to see what this monstrosity of yours sounds like."

So the next day I took some of my annual leave and we stopped off at the machine shop in Anacostia.

She fussed over the guitar like a collie over a flock of sheep, her face furrowed in a frown as she tried to get it tuned just right.

"Couldn't you just get it in relative tune? Does it have to be in concert tune?" I asked.

She looked up at me, irritated. "What do you mean?" she snapped.

"Well, relative tune means that the guitar is in tune with itself. For example, instead of E, A, D, G, B, E, you might use F#, B, E, A, C#, F#."

She frowned. "But I've got eight strings. Anyway, the notes and the overtones have to be just right. It can't be off by a single resonance."

I didn't say anything. One of the few things I've learned in this world is not to argue with a woman.

So I went for a long walk, leaving her to her work. Naturally my long walk took me to Tom's.

"Hi," he said as I walked in. "Be with you in a minute." He was aligning a couple of pieces of wood in a vise.

I wandered around the shop, smelling the sawdust and glue, touching the planed unvarnished pieces of wood, watching the strange interplay of shadows among the instruments. Memories of other guitar shops flitted through my mind, memories of the days when I thought I'd be a concert guitarist.

"Haven't seen you in a while, Dick. Been busy with that girl, Nikki?" He propped himself against a bench, pulled out a pipe, and started to tamp tobacco into it.

I grinned, embarrassed but happy, like a kid caught with his hand in the cookie jar. "Yeah. She's quite a wonderful girl."

"Yes, I guess she is." Tom lit a match and sucked in on the pipe. "But if you don't mind my saying it, Dick, she's a strange one."

"How do you mean?" I asked, feeling suddenly defensive.

"Have you looked closely at her guitar?"

I had to admit I hadn't.

"It's all wrong, Dick. It's all wrong. I'd like to hear what it sounds like when she has it strung."

"I'll tell her. But what do you mean, it's all wrong? Just because it has eight strings?"

"More than that. Here, look at these drawings. Nobody ever braced a guitar like that before. And the dimensions, the woods—well, it's just all wrong."

"Are you saying it won't play?"

"I don't know. The fretboard—the spacings are not for a twelve-tone scale. But she insisted on it."

"Well, we'll find out if it works pretty soon. She's stringing it now."

"Tell her I'd like to hear her play it when she's finished." He picked up the neck of a fiddle and began sanding it down. "Tell her I'm very curious."

I left Tom's shop and walked down to the Piraeus, the cobblestoned dock area of Annapolis town. The liquor store was still open; I bought a bottle of the red wine Nikki liked so much.

As I climbed the stairs I could hear Nikki playing. It was the most beautiful music I'd ever heard. There were resonances I'd never heard before, and the music itself was a cross between classical and jazz with an undercurrent of African rhythms, and God knows what else. She stopped on a pensive and lonely minor chord.

I waited for a moment to see if there would be any more then opened the door. She was sitting cross-legged on the floor, her face bright with a wonderingly happy smile.

"God, Nikki, that was beautiful. I've never heard anything like it. What was it? Who wrote it?"

"What? Did you hear that?" Her voice was sharp with anger.

"Yes. I was just outside the door."

"Why didn't you come in? Why were you snooping on me?"

"I wasn't snooping on you." I had never seen Nikki angry before and I couldn't understand it now. "I just didn't want to interrupt you."

"Well, you shouldn't have done it. It was wrong."

"All right. I'm sorry." I was beginning to get a little hot under the collar myself.

"Don't do it again."

"All right, I won't," I snapped.

She got control of herself again. "I'm sorry, Dick. I didn't mean to yell at you. I just, well, I just don't like people snooping on me. It makes me nervous."

"I'm sorry. I won't do it again. Honest." She smiled at me and how could I stay angry? We hugged each other and she cried a little and we both said "I'm sorry" again about half a dozen times until we almost got angry again over who should be sorry, and then we were laughing, partly out of the sheer relief of having weathered our first real argument.

"By the way," I said, putting the wine into the refrigerator, "Tom would like to hear you play."

"No."

"What do you mean, 'no'? You owe it to him, Nikki. After all, he was good enough to make the guitar for you."

"I don't know. Let me think about it."

"He really would be surprised. I don't think either of us expected it to be such a beautiful instrument."

"Please, Dick. Let's talk about something else."

I should have dropped the subject there. "Just tell me what that was you played."

"It's called 'Concerto for Guitar'." Her voice was tense.

"It must be recent. I've never heard it before."

"Very."

"Who wrote it?"

"I... I can't tell you. I forget. Maybe I never knew. I don't know."

"I don't think you want to tell me and I'd like to know why."

"It's none of your goddamned business!"

It was two days before we were talking to each other again without any tenseness.

❧ ◄ ► ❧

Nikki gave in and agreed to play the guitar for Tom but she insisted that he come over to our apartment. That was fine with me, because he had never been there before. He said nothing when he came in, but he nodded his head in approval.

Nikki gave him a glass of wine and he finally said, "The way you two are acting makes me feel I should bow to Mecca or something. What's with all this tiptoeing around like a couple of mice?"

"Sorry," Nikki said.

"Wait till you hear her play the guitar," I said.

Tom sat in the easy chair while I perched on the edge of the bed. Nikki sat on the floor, spent a few moments tuning the guitar, and finally began playing.

This time I recognized the piece: Tarrega's *Recuerdo de la Alhambra*. It wasn't nearly as beautiful or lovely as the piece she had played earlier, which was still rattling around in my head, but it was the most enchanting version of Tarrega I'd ever heard.

When she was finished, I asked her who had transcribed it.

"What do you mean?"

"Well, that was written for six strings, not eight."

"Oh," she said, as if it had not occurred to her. "I don't know."

"Maybe it was the fellow who wrote that other piece, the one I first heard you play."

She sat there, cradling her guitar, looking strangely miserable. "I don't know. Maybe. I just don't know." She was very near to tears.

"Play it for Tom," I suggested.

She shook her head.

"Why not?"

"I can't," she cried, and fled into the bathroom.

Tom drained his glass and left a few minutes later. I apologized to him.

"Don't blame yourself, Dick. She's a strange girl."

"Hey, Nikki," I said, after he left. "I'm sorry. I didn't mean to embarrass you."

She came out of the bathroom, smiling bravely. "It's all right, Dick. Just don't ask me to play that piece again."

"All right. But why?"

"Just don't. Please. I can't tell you why."

Then she sidetracked me, and it was no longer a time for words.

෨◀▷෧

A few nights later, we were sitting around, reading, watching television, acting very much like the old married couple, when she asked me to go out and get a bottle of wine.

"Are we out already?"

"I think so."

"Okay, let's go. It's a nice night for a walk."

"Could you go without me? I don't feel like getting dressed."

"What do you mean? That's silly. You can go as you are." She was wearing the same pale yellow dress she had worn the first time I saw her.

"I don't know. I just would rather stay in, that's all. Do you mind?"

I started to get angry again, but caught myself before I had said a word. "No. It's all right. I'll be back before you know I'm gone."

It was a beautiful night, the breeze off the bay keeping the summer heat at a tolerable level. The middies were walking around in groups of young men or paired off with town girls. The older townspeople were doing their evening shopping and teenagers were looking aimlessly for something to do.

The Piraeus was alive with the traffic that always piles up there, and pleasure boats and cruisers were aswarm with people. I didn't hurry but I didn't dawdle either. I bought the wine and walked back past Tom's shop, but I didn't go in.

Nikki wasn't there when I got back. I thought she was in the bathroom so I hollered, "I'm back," and went into the kitchenette to open the wine. I poured a couple of glasses and sat down to watch TV.

That's when I noticed the bathroom door was open. I called her name but that was ridiculous, for there was no place for her to hide. But I did find a note:

Dick—

I'm sorry to leave you like this, without warning.

But, if I didn't, you'd try to follow me, and I can't have that. Don't wait for me to come back or try to find me— you'll be wasting your time.

It's not that I don't love you, but it just wasn't meant to be. I can't explain.

৯◄►৻

I raced out of the apartment and, after darting around the streets and alleys for a few minutes, stopping people to ask them if they'd seen a girl in a yellow dress and, getting nothing but amused smiles, I paused to think.

I didn't know how long she'd been gone but she probably had packed and gone as soon as I left. It wouldn't have taken her more than ten minutes so she had no more had a half-hour start on me.

I got my car and began driving around, stopping whenever I saw a short girl in a yellow dress.

I was driving down St. John's Street, beginning to believe that I'd never see her again, when I saw a girl in a yellow dress crossing the legislative parking lot to the road which led out of town to Route 50 and Washington. She was carrying a strange-looking guitar.

I stopped, backed up, stalled, turned around, and reached Bladen Street in time to see a Mustang stop to pick her up.

I stayed behind, watching the Mustang's taillights, my chest tight and tense. My eyes were squinted up and they hurt as if they wanted to cry but didn't know how.

The Mustang followed the road to Route 50 and headed for Washington. It pulled over to the side of the road a few miles later, at the bridge over South River.

There was nothing I could do—by the time I had caught up, the Mustang had pulled away and Nikki was running across the road, over the parkway dividing the traffic lanes, and into the woods on the other side of the highway.

I pulled over at the same place where the Mustang had and followed her. There was a path through the woods on the bluff high over South River. The full moon shining through the trees made it easy to follow. I could hear her ahead of me, running through the woods, making no attempt to be quiet.

Since I was able to follow her without making much noise, I was aware when she stopped.

"Chal?" I heard her say. There was no answer.

I crept forward, careful to be silent.

Then I heard the guitar—it made a flurry of notes, a quick melodic riff, and stopped. I heard a man's voice: I couldn't make out what he said, but I heard Nikki's name. My chest grew tight again.

"Chal, everything went all wrong. We're far too early; I broke the guitar and had to make a new one. I was afraid the overtones wouldn't be right and the gate wouldn't open. And I met Richard Radcliffe. Richard Radcliffe! And I loused up everything, Chal; I completely changed everything! What'll we do?"

The man, Chal, I guess, said something else, in a questioning tone of voice. I was able to make out what he was saying, but I couldn't understand a word. It was in some strange language. He used Nikki's name twice, and he seemed to be trying to calm her down.

She answered him in the same language, a little hesitantly at first, then rapidly, fluently.

All this time, I had been creeping quietly up the path. Now I could see her: she was in a small clearing in the woods, her pale yellow dress glowing in the moonlight. I couldn't see the man at all.

He said something else but I still couldn't understand him, though every word was perfectly clear. And I had no idea where he was.

Nikki said nothing, just stood there, shaking her head.

The man said something, questioningly.

Nikki answered and her voice sounded faintly choked. Then she said something else, louder and more sharply, but the note of despair in her voice made me want to rush out and hold her.

Her dress seemed to glitter in the moonlight, growing brighter and then fading. It seemed as though I could see through her. The moon was shining right through, glowing on the grass beyond her.

And she was gone.

I rushed into the clearing, calling her name, but she was gone, guitar and all. There was no sign she had ever been there.

I spend very little time in my apartment now; I just sleep there. I spend a lot of time watching the sailboats on the Severn River. I talked Tom into making another eight-stringed guitar and the people in Anacostia are making another set of strings for me.

And I keep walking the streets of Annapolis town, looking for a girl in a pale yellow dress, walking the streets of Annapolis town with the notes to a concerto for eight-stringed guitar running through my mind.

STELLA BLUE

It all rolls into one in the end; all the years combine and melt into a dream. The song is in the wind, stellar or temporal, and we drift like separate atoms in the tangled skein of DNA. If I make sense, you understand more than I do. My tale is twisted in time, flotsam on the stream, prisoner to the vagaries of the current.

Her name was Stella Blue. It was other things as well, but when Garcia first saw her, her name was Stella Blue. He didn't know her tale then but, if he had, perhaps it would have made no difference to him.

She was playing guitar in the Row Jimmy. Once the eyes of the world had been on her, stripping her naked, exposing all her secret places, then passing on to look for others to slake their insatiable scrutiny and curiosity. But that is another tale, and not a very interesting one. It is replayed every day with more melodramatic variants.

In the wake of that flood, she had been tossed up, a piece of driftwood, in the Row Jimmy where she performed nightly, all the rest stored and forgotten in the attics of her life.

Garcia was young then, not yet the dire and fearsome wolf he was to become, and one of the best classical autar players in the world. He was a brilliant technician, flawlessly following the written line in all its complexity. But the improvisational confidence needed to play *grilly* and rock was not yet his, although he practiced in secret; more important, his line was cold, emotionless, and unfeeling. It was a common criticism, and one Garcia didn't understand.

Not until that night when he stopped for a sniff at the Row Jimmy and heard Stella Blue playing in the corner for mere nixons. He had always scoffed at the guitar as a derelict of time, maddeningly lacking in complexity, and totally incapable of nuances and subtleties.

Then he heard Stella Blue.

A broken angel sang from her guitar, through all the broken dreams and vanished hopes. He heard the winds of time; he felt the weight of agelessness upon the immortals. Her guitar was crying like the wind, down every lonely street that had ever been. She played the legendary music of Radcliffe as Garcia had never heard it played before, the simple uncomplex music Radcliffe had composed before he and the mythical Tom had invented the first autar. She played it with a despair and sense of loss that struck even the emotionless Garcia.

"Who is she?" he asked the tender when he found his voice again.

"Stella Blue."

"Is that her real name?"

The tender shrugged. "Stella Blue she calls herself; Stella Blue we credit her; and Stella Blue the puter accepts. Stella Blue she is now, whatever she was before. We don't question here, stranger."

Stella Blue finished playing and left the stage. Garcia shouldered his way through the crowd, oblivious to the insults he was collecting, and reached the girl before she could leave by a side door, grabbing her by the elbow.

"Can I buy you a sniff, Miss?"

She pulled away from him. "No, thank you." Her depthless gray eyes stared past him as if he wasn't there.

"Look, please join me, Miss. I..."

A gorilla stepped between him and Stella Blue, and she drifted through the doorway.

"You don't hear the lady, stranger?"

"I didn't mean anything. I'm Garcia; I could make her famous."

"And pulp I could make you."

Garcia knew he had lost the battle.

৯◄►৩

His console was of little help. "No Stella Blue is listed," it told him.

He had half-expected it. He stood at the window, staring out at the luminescent river flowing several dozen floors below him, underlighting the bridges and buildings. "No Stella Blue?" he repeated. "Nowhere?"

"No listing in the public file."

Garcia picked up his favorite autar and keyed a basic grilly progression, playing his own counterpoint on the strings while the computer adjusted its own timing and harmony to his melody. After a few bars, he began plucking strings idly, hitting keys at random while the computer tried franticly to find a pattern in his idle strumming. He put it down. Even the autar couldn't calm him tonight.

The display case containing the ancient autar that had supposedly been played by Radcliffe himself caught his eye. The old instrument was one of Garcia's prized possessions, a conversation piece, a status symbol. As an instrument, Garcia found it hopelessly inadequate, barely more complex than a mere guitar.

He unlocked the case and took out the ancient instrument.

There was only one fretboard and the computer used punched cards rather than keyed input. It was much more limited than a modern autar's computer. Garcia turned the instrument over idly in his hands, oddly moved by this link with the past in a way he had never felt before. It had been only a few years earlier a timedipper had stumbled across Radcliffe and thus proved he had actually existed, although certainly many of the stories about him were apocryphal. The girl had played several Radcliffe compositions and others Garcia hadn't recognized, probably her own.

He inserted one of the punched cards that had come with the instrument into its reader and powered it up. A steady rhythm with a treble harmony began. This instrument was not one to follow the performer; the player had to follow the computer. Garcia began to play, amused by the prospect. It was not as easy as he had expected, but the music was good; he made very few mistakes the first time through, and none the second. Then he began playing the strings separately, two against the bass, three against the treble, another against the bass, building a complex line that the original designer of the instrument would never have thought possible.

At last, contented and pleased with himself, he powered the instrument down. There had been resonances in the wood that he would never have been able to obtain with a modern instrument. Gently, like a lover with a newfound mate, he caressed the instrument, turning it over again, examining it for the first time in years. The builder's name, Raymond, was on the head. He wondered who Raymond was, what he had looked like, what his last name was. Perhaps he had been a friend of Radcliffe's; if Radcliffe had truly played this instrument, then maybe he had been. Garcia toyed with the idea of asking the timedippers to check into it, but he knew it was too trivial for such a waste of energy.

He returned the autar to its case, promising himself to play it more often in the future.

It was two nights before he could get back to the Row Jimmy, and he half-expected she would be gone when he got there. But she was still on the tiny corner stage, as if she had never left. He tried to reach her while she was still playing, but the same gorilla stopped him just before he reached the stage.

"The performer's not to be disturbed, stranger."

"I just want to request a song."

"Requests she doesn't take."

"I'd like her to play Radcliffe's Concerto for Guitar," Garcia insisted, hoping she would hear him.

"Requests she doesn't take," the gorilla repeated.

"Just this once," Garcia said. "Radcliffe's Concerto for Guitar," he repeated, louder.

She looked grayly at him and stopped playing. "I don't play that anymore," she said softly.

The sadness in her voice, just this side of tears, touched the heartless Garcia. "I'm sorry," he said.

"Requests she doesn't take," the gorilla said. "I told you."

Garcia stumbled away.

He left the fashionably shabby neighborhood of the Row Jimmy and returned to the faceless façade of the main city, going straight to Computer Central. A computer aide, wired directly into the computer, took his request for Stella Blue's true name.

"That information is restricted," the aide said. "You are not on the authorized list."

Garcia looked up at the aide, whose torso disappeared into a metal-bright cabinet that placed him slightly higher than Garcia. "But she does have another name?" he asked.

"That I don't know, and I couldn't tell you if I did. I can only tell you that all information on Stella Blue is restricted." The aide looked stonily at him from copper-colored eyes. "Just as all information on the private life of a classical autar player known only as Garcia is restricted. You understand, I'm sure."

"But that's just it! I'm sure she'd love to talk to me if I could get to her. I can make her famous."

"You're not authorized."

"But don't you understand? I'm Garcia."

The aide looked at him distantly. "There is no more I can do for you, sir. If you wish to discuss it with my superiors, you can key in a request at the public console to your left. Next, please."

But fame, like rank, has its privileges, and information sources, even if they are computers, have their back doors. Garcia had not really expected any better treatment at Computer Central, any more than he had expected to learn anything when he had originally queried the computer from his own console. But he needed to make the attempt, if only to convince himself that he was forced to take the next step.

He entered the office of his last teacher, Bwire, who was now in charge of the conservatory. He outlined the story to the old man and waited while Bwire looked at him with a steadiness that unnerved the rock-steady Garcia.

"I've never seen you like this," Bwire said in a strong crystalline voice. "For ten years I've known you, my boy, and never has anyone or anything touched that granite heart of yours."

"That's not true," Garcia protested. "The autar has been my life, my dream. It's been my heart, my soul. You know that."

"A cold, passionate love, though, it has been."

Garcia shook his head. "I don't understand that. You're wrong. You're like those people who say my playing lacks passion."

The old man paused again to look steadily at Garcia. He smiled. "Perhaps," he said, almost under his breath. "Perhaps. Well, tell me, my boy, is your... *feeling* for this Stella Blue anything like your love for the autar?"

"No, of course not. This is irrational. I can't control it. It's eating me up. I don't understand it."

Bwire made a steeple with his hands. "I see." The smile reached his eyes. "Hopes I had for you, Garcia. My best pupil you were. The greatest autar player ever I once thought you would be. Lately, I have not been so sure."

"What do you mean? Of course, I'm the best. Everyone says so."

"Not everyone. Never mind. My mind I have changed again. There is still hope for you."

"You're talking in riddles," Garcia grumbled, thinking the old man was becoming senile.

"Never mind. Why did you tell me all this? I know you better than to think you came here just to unburden your heart."

Garcia shifted uncomfortably in his chair. "Well, I know you have access to restricted information..." Bwire raised a white eyebrow. "I mean, in your position, as head of the school..."

"Some restricted information you want me to obtain for you?" the old man asked quietly.

"Just to find out where Stella Blue lives. What her real name is."

Bwire looked at Garcia for a long moment, longer than any of his previous pauses. At last he smiled a quiet, secret, enigmatic smile and nodded his head. "Perhaps I will. Perhaps I will." The statement was barely more than a whisper, more to himself than to Garcia. He stared at his desk for another moment then turned to his console and keyed in a request. He watched the display, which was hidden from Garcia.

There was something different in his gaze when he looked again at Garcia, a something mixed of pity and indecision. "Do you know who N'kwenze is?" Garcia shook his head. "You should. You're remarkably lacking in general knowledge outside of your own narrow interests, do you know that?"

"Does it matter?"

"It does, but you won't believe me. If you did, that question you wouldn't have to ask."

"Look, just tell me her name, where she lives. That's all I ask."

"The timedipper who discovered Radcliffe was N'kwenze. She fell in love with him and he with her. After she returned to our time, several pieces for the guitar he wrote and then the autar invented. Suicide, he committed ten years after she left him, still despondent over her disappearance."

Garcia said nothing. Bwire had always been given to rambling but it seemed to have gotten worse with age. Sooner or later, he knew, Bwire would give him the information he sought.

"N'kwenze is Stella Blue," Bwire said quietly.

Garcia didn't think there was any place in the city more decrepit than the area where the Row Jimmy was located, but he was wrong. Garcia had grown up in sheltered affluence, a prodigy whose every whim was carefully considered, often fulfilled.

Where N'kwenze lived was centuries old, with combination locks instead of personal locks. Parts of the buildings, like parts of Garcia's ancient autar, were made of wood. The bright shadowless streets and boulevards of the main city to which he was accustomed had not yet reached this section. Shadows seemed to creep out of corners, attempting to catch unsuspecting passersby. The buildings disappeared in the haze above the streetlamps. The darkness called to Garcia, lured him to explorations, even as it frightened him with visions of violence.

He found her address and rode the ancient elevator to her floor. There was no doorchime or voicebox but Bwire had anticipated that and had explained the ancient tradition of "knocking" to Garcia.

Garcia "knocked."

"Who is it?"

"You don't know me. I saw you at the Row Jimmy a couple of nights ago..."

"How did you find me?" The voice, which had been soft and timorous at first, was now hard and distant.

"I'm Garcia. I have connections."

"Go away."

Garcia wondered if the gorilla was with her. "I know it's no business of mine, but I just want to talk with you."

"I don't want to talk with anyone."

"I'm not leaving."

"I'll call the police."

Garcia laughed. "You forget who I am, and who you are."

"There are other people who will help me."

"You'd call them?" It was a bluff; she didn't seem like the kind of person who'd intentionally have someone else hurt.

After a long pause, she asked, "What do you want to talk to me about?"

For a moment, Garcia was at a loss for words, since he really didn't know himself. At last he said, "Your playing. You're... you're incredible."

"You can hear me tonight."

"It's not that. Please. Please talk to me."

He heard her sigh, then the rattle of a chain being released, another, and the door opened.

Her room belonged to another century. An old-fashioned double bed, with rumpled sheets, dominated the room. A rickety old chair, a set of drawers, and a flat television were the other main pieces of furniture. A picture of a smiling young man was on the small bedside table. There was no computer console.

She sat down on the bed and motioned him over to the chair. As he sat down, he noticed the guitar case next to the chair. She watched him as he stared at the room.

"It's Twentieth Century American. Latter half," she said at last. "I used to be a timedipper," she said quietly.

"I know."

"You know?" she asked sharply.

"You're N'kwenze, the one who found Radcliffe."

"Then you know everything."

The despair, the resignation in her voice, touched the wakening Garcia. "I don't know what you mean."

"Please, leave me alone."

"I can help you."

"I don't need your help. I don't need anyone's help. Dick is dead, and I might as well be."

"I don't understand. Why don't you go back?"

"And change the timestream? It can't be done. And even if it could, they wouldn't let me." She got up. "Here. Have you seen this?" She picked up a cassette.

"What is it?"

She inserted it into her TV and turned down the lights. Garcia watched as a man grown old and haggard before his time played an ancient autar. His technique was clumsy and simplistic, but there was a raw power that Garcia almost envied. When he was finished, the audience that had been watching him applauded for a long time. He stood in front of them, his gray-streaked head bowed. The camera moved closer and Garcia could see the lines, the crow's feet, the despair.

"That was Dick's last concert," she said. "Another timedipper attended it while on another assignment and made that tape for me."

"I see." The performance had affected him much as Stella Blue's guitar playing had.

"He wasn't even forty-five." She turned away from him, her body tense, her hands balled into fists. Then she said quietly, almost inaudibly, "He committed suicide the next day."

"You can't live in the past," he said, wondering why he was doing this, why he was in this decrepit room, trying to reach a really quite plain woman when there were plenty of others who would beg for his attention.

"Is that what you came here for? To tell me that I can't live in the past?"

"No. I... I..." The glib Garcia was at a loss for words, not quite knowing what to say.

"What did you *really* come here for?"

Garcia sighed. "I'm not sure. You just fascinate me. I'm not sure why."

"Necrophilia," she said, bitterly. "You're just like the others."

"No, no, that's not it at all. I knew nothing about any of this when I first saw you. But you just... you're different somehow and your music disturbs me, touches me somehow."

She smiled sadly. "I see," she said, nodding her head. "I think it would be best if you left now."

"No, please. When can I see you again?"

"Never."

⊱◄►⊰

She did not return to the Row Jimmy and when Garcia went to her room again, she was gone. He enlisted Bwire's help once more.

"It's you again," she said when he arrived at her new address, which was not much different from her previous quarters.

"I'll hunt you to the ends of the Earth."

"That won't be necessary."

Their conversation was as fruitless as the previous one and Garcia was on the street again after a few minutes. He stood there, tasting the icy knife-edge of impending violence that seemed to hang over this section of town. He was becoming used to it now and he no longer felt the urge to hasten back to more familiar territory. The shadows and ancient lighting reached into him and touched deep anticipations and memory traces. Ghosts of the past beckoned to him from the shadows, and echoes of forgotten songs lingered in the air.

The door to Stella Blue's building opened and the girl came out. She did not see Garcia standing in the shadows. He started forward then remembered their fruitless meeting and stayed back, following her, keeping to the shadows, though she never looked back.

She came to the river and dove in, pausing only to take off her shoes. Garcia thought of the strong undertow of the sluggish main current, stripped, and dove in after her.

If there were any words exchanged between the two of them in that cold and phosphorescent river, they are lost and forgotten. Garcia caught up to her as she was tiring, tried to get her to head back to shore. But a third joined them, an inanimate third, one of the rivercleaners, its maw full of teeth and blades for the shredding of large river debris. He tried to pull the girl away from its path but she struggled. The suction action of the rivercleaner pulled them inexorably into its mouth, spinning them around each other until Garcia hit its edge. He felt as if a razor was cutting him apart, then he was pulled free. Pain washed over him and he knew no more.

ço⟨⟩ço

He awoke at last after a jumbled series of vague memories of anesthetic smells, of green-masked surgeons, of fresh-scrubbed rubber and plastic. He awoke to the smiling, seamed face of a doctor.

"Ah, me Jocko, it is good to have you back with the living," the doctor said expansively. "'Tis not to worry. An arm, an arm. What's an arm?"

"An arm?" Garcia asked groggily.

"So much worse it could have been. 'Tis hard we worked for such a famous man. 'Tis not to worry. See?" He took off his own arm and thrust it under Garcia's nose. "Only your prosthetician will know for sure." He turned the arm around for Garcia's inspection, admiring it himself. "More delicacy, more control, more finesse than the biological model." He thrust another arm in Garcia's face. This one terminated in a surgical saw, a pair of pincers, and a surgical needle. "'Tis a poorer surgeon I'd be elsewise. To cut, to slice, to sew, so." He slashed the air in Garcia's face with the surgical arm, then stood back and smiled warmly. "So you see, me lad, 'tis no tragedy. 'Tis a blessing, in truth."

Bwire was sadder, more morose, when he visited Garcia. "Her name I should never have given you. A one-armed autar player? My hopes, my dreams, all dashed and shattered."

And then the girl visited him, a bitter smile on her face.

"You saved my life, didn't you?" he asked. "Why?"

The bitter smile turned on itself and a fleeting pain crossed her face. "I killed one man already. I couldn't let it happen again." She stared at the floor, looking like a shattered and forgotten doll. Garcia wanted desperately to embrace her, to hold her, console her, make her happy."

And with that desire, he remembered the stump of an arm at his shoulder, and he shared her bitterness. "Maybe you should have let me die," he said.

She looked at him, full of an understanding he had lacked. "Maybe. But I couldn't do it again. Anyway, your doctor says your new arm will be better than the original one. You'll have more control than ever before."

"It won't be the same," he said.

"No. I suppose not."

She walked along a river of melted sherbet: lime and raspberry eddied in scallops beside the sluggish main current of phosphorescent orange streaked with a rich brown chocolate.

It glowed on the underside of the bridge, lighting her face from below.

Who could know her thoughts as she stood on that bridge? Perhaps she remembered a time when rivers still ran clear, when there were a still a few people who walked slowly and savored the salt breeze, not rushing madly in search of new experiences already old. Perhaps she remembered a time of gentleness and love, the warmth of a strong man with a red mustache, the weakness of a sandy-haired dreamer. Perhaps she thought that if she had wings, the turgid air would support her despite the claims of physicists. But she had no wings and it is more likely she knew her flight would be that of a stone.

When they told Garcia of her death, his face took on a granitic mien it never again quite lost. He turned around and walked away.

A colleague found him several months later, playing guitar in a shabby club called the Row Jimmy. His playing was awkward, clumsy, and ragged... but it had a poignancy and depth his autar-playing had never had.

Ideally, the story should end there, but life is not as tidy and neat as art. Garcia was more stable than Radcliffe or N'kwenze. Six months later, he was back on the classical stage, and no one could deny, however grudgingly, he was now the best classical autar player. His line was still as technically clean as ever, but now there was something more, something deeper; call it passion, feeling, soul, or whatever you will.

Nor did it end there. Always a man of ambition, Garcia was now a man possessed. He reached into other realms, mastering all varieties of autar-playing, from grilly to pop and rock and beyond. And he tossed off women like whiskey chasers, with a cruelty that was somehow gentle.

Thus do legends feed upon themselves. Thus does the timestream bend back upon itself, like a DNA strand forming sulfide bridges between amino acids. Thus has it been; thus it will be. In the end, it's just a song, and nothing comes for free.

TIME'S FOOL

Chapter 1

As Garcia moved through the party, waves of conversation, like the somnolent disharmonies of Vlatko's "Modular" symphony, crested on the autarist's ears. He stopped to flirt briefly with a young synthesist who wore one of Amiloun's programmable gowns. This one writhed about the young synthesist's body slowly, changing colors and iridescing, revealing and concealing, its movements programmed to display its host's finest features to their best advantage.

Justin Mead gestured to Garcia from the other side of the room and Garcia moved over to his side. Justin's knotted and gnarled hand carried the flute he played so beautifully. "How about a duet?"

"Certainly." Garcia picked up a nearby guitar. For a few moments, the two friends weaved melodies and harmonies, Garcia dropping into straight rhythm while Justin's flute swooped and soared, spreading crystalline notes through the party, then Justin played low throaty soft warbles while Garcia plucked arpeggios, triples, and two- and three-note chords from his instrument.

When they were done, the people clustered around them applauded. Justin looked at Garcia. "Your choice," he said.

Garcia held up his hand. "Maybe later."

Justin's creased face became even more lined with concern. "Is something wrong? You don't usually settle for just one song."

"Nothing's wrong, Justin."

But as he moved away from his friend, Garcia wasn't so certain. He had hoped playing music with Justin would quell the undercurrent of dissatisfaction that refused to identify itself; instead, it had seemed to intensify the feeling. There had been no satisfaction in music well-played, once again sharing the moment with Justin. It seemed he had done it too many times before.

He stood at his false fireplace, staring at the simulated fire, the faint scent of cedar drifting past his nostrils. The glass of dark cognac in his hand was forgotten, and the party's hum, the polychords of disconnected conversations, went past him, unheard.

"Don't look so sad, Garcia." A pretty girl ran her hand up his real arm. Garcia smiled briefly at her and turned away. Garcia did not often turn away from a pretty girl.

Shrill laughter burst over the conversational hum, like a discordant trumpet solo.

Garcia's agent, Renard, was talking to a moderately pretty woman, one of the few at the party Garcia did not already know. Her sharp-featured face had an alert, lively expression he found appealing, although a number of the women present were considerably more attractive than she.

"Have you met Shaara yet?" Renard asked.

"No, I don't think so. She must have slipped in when I wasn't looking."

She smiled at him warmly. "I'm pleased to meet you." Her handshake was firm and unfeminine.

"Shaara," Garcia repeated.

"That's right."

"She wanted to meet you, Garcia, so I brought her along. She's Muenstretiger's daughter."

"Muenstretiger." The name was familiar, but Garcia couldn't place it.

"He's the chairman of Merck and Muenstretiger. Pharmaceuticals."

"Oh, yes." It was the largest of the pharmaceutical firms.

"She's made a bit of a reputation on her own, as a plastic artist. She's having an exhibition of her mobile art down at Dr. Hawk's."

Garcia turned to Shaara. "This place must appear rather poor to you."

"I'm afraid I *do* find it a bit tasteless." Shaara's smile softened the impact of her words. "I really had expected better of you."

They were standing in the doorway to Garcia's bedroom. A varibed, now dialed to soft, dominated one corner of the room. Ancient prints, some of them erotic, adorned the earthy red-brown walls. The floor was covered with a shaggy Oriental carpet heavily laced with muted black and orange designs.

"You seem to be obsessed with royal themes." She looked around the main room, where Garcia's friends were chatting, drinking, playing instruments, and singing. That room was sunk about two feet below the level of his bedroom, so Garcia's entrances were always down to it, majestic and royal. He had often enjoyed "holding court" in that room, sitting in the conspicuously Spartan chair in front of the fireplace, listening to the conversation, and only occasionally deigning to speak a few words or to play a short melody on his guitar. He would sit there regally, smiling on his favorites, tossing tidbits into the unreal fire. It was all a game, really; he consciously realized that for the first time as he looked over Shaara's shoulder.

The whole thing now seemed devoid of interest and savor. It was a thing of childhood, something to be put aside. But what was there to take its place?

"What are you scowling about? I didn't mean to offend you."

Broken rudely out of his reverie, Garcia stuttered for a moment. "Oh, you didn't offend me. I was just thinking." He gestured at the main room. "Perhaps you're right. I *do* seem to have an obsession with royalty. Medieval royalty at that."

All the main room's pretensions now hung over him. He had once pictured it as a medieval Spanish castle, with banners and standards hanging from the walls, a few wolfhounds wandering among the guests, flagons of wine, stone walls and roaring fires, with balladeers and full-skirted women roaming through the halls.

Instead, he had a meager, unreal fire, a carefully random selection of chairs and seats, plush rugs, and a retinue of sycophants. He, himself, was the balladeer, the minstrel, whose artificial fingers played melodies with more precision and feeling than anyone else had ever done before.

Or was he merely the fool?

"It *does* kind of suit you."

"How's that?"

"I have this picture of you, an overblown romantic fantasy, I'm afraid, where you're standing on a bluff overlooking the ocean, wearing a cape that's blowing in the wind."

Garcia frowned. It was too close to his own fantasies for comfort.

"You don't like that."

"You're right. It *is* a bit overblown."

She touched his arm. "Do you... do you mind talking about this?"

Garcia smiled. She had been touching his real arm. "There's not much to say about that one."

"There's not? I thought..." She stopped, blushing, as she realized her mistake. "I... I... but the other one looks so real."

Garcia reached up to his right shoulder and detached the arm. His sleeve hung empty as he handed the arm to the woman. She took it gingerly. "But it's warm!"

"They can do wonders with electronics and plastic." Garcia was uncomfortable. The arms were all part of him; he felt naked without one, no matter how much clothing he might be wearing.

She handed it back to him and he quickly locked it back into place.

"I knew my father was doing wonderful things in the prosthetics line. I've used some of his techniques myself in some of my sculptures. But I hadn't realized he'd gone this far."

"Well, they're quite expensive, believe me. At least, for a musician. And I need several of them."

"How many do you have?"

"Five."

"What do you need that many for?"

"I have two performance arms. They look just like my social arms but they're more sensitive and complicated. And, of course, they're programmed to play the autar. The fingers are more flexible and I have a finer sense of touch and more delicacy. But I wouldn't dare shake hands with them, and I certainly wouldn't do anything with them that required any strength."

"You play quite well with that arm." She indicated the one he was wearing.

"It's an all-purpose arm, what's called a social arm. It's capable of doing just about anything that can be done with a real arm. So I can play guitar quite competently with it. Or autar."

"That accounts for three of your arms. What about the other two?"

"I have another social arm, a spare, and the other one is for doing delicate manual labor. Instead of fingers, it has tools, test probes, and other appendages. It even has a kind of an eye."

"An eye? What on Earth for?"

"It's very handy for working inside my autar. That's what the arm is for, working on my instruments."

"I'd think you would have someone else do that for you. You certainly can afford it."

"Yes, but working on my own instruments helps me understand them better, learning their limitations, and how to work with them instead of against them. It's another facet of being a performer, one that many entertainers ignore."

"I see... I think."

"Don't worry about it." He held his hand out. She took it and they descended to the main room. The staged effect of their return to the party made Garcia very uncomfortable.

Chapter 2

At last Garcia was alone; everyone had gone and he was finally able to stand still and think. But his thoughts wouldn't hold still long enough for him to grab onto them.

He walked to the doorway and leaned his weight against it, both hands against the sills. The main room was empty; there was no one in it to whom he could play lord. It was just as well. He was wearing only a pair of tight-fitting, bright red trunks now, and they looked ludicrous on his stocky body, emphasizing his nascent obesity. His stomach hung slightly over the trunks in rolls of fat that refused to go away. He thought of Justin's slender, reed-like body with rueful envy.

His hair was tousled and unkempt, sticking out in all directions. He fancied that he looked like a Spanish don surveying his domain, and he was fully aware of it and did nothing to change his mien. He was also aware he was his own best audience and that he enjoyed these little games, like a little child playing at being lost adrift on the sea, making a raft out of a few chairs and a seat.

Ordinarily he could draw on his emotions for the power and strength that poured out of him when he was in the spotlight, even on his unhappiness and uneasiness, but now there was a restlessness that underlined his unhappiness in a manner he couldn't enjoy.

He picked up a glass of wine and stared into it. It was calm and unperturbed but, when he started to swirl it, a vortex formed in the middle. Meanwhile, at the edges of the wine, eddies formed and broke up, battling each other, so transient that they were barely formed before they destroyed themselves, while the central vortex remained coherent. It was like his own thoughts and emotions, moving too fast for identification, breaking up and reforming even as he tried to examine them, Heisenberg's principle in action among the electro-chemical synapses of his mind.

He sipped the wine. It was warm and flat, as his life had become. Its edge was gone. At first he had enjoyed the attentions of his meteoric rise to fame. No one else approached his mastery of the autar, which some claimed to be one of the most complex and difficult instruments ever invented. Nor had his rise to fame been slowed by an incident that had occurred early in his career, an event that already was beginning to attain mythic status.

It had only been five years since Garcia, already established as a performer, met Stella Blue, a timedipper who had encountered the composer Radcliffe while on a research trip, and fallen in love with him. She had returned to her own time (and Garcia's), been cashiered from the timedippers, and was making her living as a guitarist in a tiny club in the *barraque* when Garcia first heard her, and fell in love with her and her sad, plaintive music. His entreaties had only resulted in her attempted suicide; in saving her, Garcia had lost his arm. Its replacement was more sensitive and versatile than the original, but it was not that which was primarily responsible for his subsequent meteoric career. Stella Blue had committed suicide while Garcia was recovering and the whole experience and its emotions found their outlet in his music. A new dimension was added to Garcia's performances, which had been clean and faultless before, but colorless, without fire. Now an inner fire burned and consumed his performances.

Was it that same fire that now was reaching into his private life, refusing to let him alone? Or was the fire dying instead, with its embers winking out, leaving him alone and hollow, like a deaf musician? Garcia stared into the wine and wondered. At last he put it down and walked back to the bedroom, pulling aside an Oriental tapestry and unlocking the door behind it.

This room, thus uncovered, lacked the opulence of Garcia's other rooms. It was antiseptic and sound-absorbent. In airtight cabinets on one wall of the room were Garcia's instruments: the ancient autar supposedly invented by Radcliffe himself; the guitar that Stella Blue had been playing when Garcia first met her. Two other modern-day autars were in their cases under the display cabinets. Recording machines lined another wall, with inset directional microphones which could be swiveled to point wherever needed.

In a corner of the cabinet, near Stella Blue's guitar, were pictures of her and Radcliffe, and a tape of Radcliffe's last performance, a clumsy and awkward performance, but one with more power and fire than Garcia had ever been able to summon.

He touched a spot on the one blank wall in the room and part of that wall went transparent, revealing an awesome view of the city. Lights stretched out in front of Garcia and to the sides, more or less orderly, for most of the residents were asleep. But the lights of all-night establishments, factories and power stations, still burned, forming blocks of luminescence among the strings of street lights. Bridges were necklaces of light, like spider webs hung with morning dew, and the river flowed sluggishly, glowing faintly, underneath them. It was there Stella Blue had drowned herself; it was there Garcia had lost his arm to the mouth of a river cleaner while stopping her first attempt.

He unlocked the cabinet and took out her guitar. He had scorned such simple instruments before he met her, but since her death he had mastered it, marveling at the raw emotions it evoked, and at the nuances he was able to attain with such a basic instrument. He had been so smug and self-satisfied before he met her, completely oblivious to a whole world of emotions and abilities that were just outside the periphery of his knowledge. It had been a simple world, but he would not go back to it if he could; it seemed a drab and colorless life, atonal and monotone, compared the kaleidoscopic life he now knew.

He played the guitar for fifteen minutes, beginning with a simple progression of single notes that rapidly wove themselves into a complex cascade of harmonies and counterpoint, then dying back to the simple progression of single notes. It was his farewell to Stella Blue, the only composition he had ever written which he had never performed publicly, a hymn of thanks to her, and a paean.

He returned to the main room, poured himself a large glass of wine, turned off the lights and tried to drink himself to sleep. Stars and planets played gently on his ceiling and soft music played from the wall. But it was still a long time to dawn.

Chapter 3

The decayed and ancient face of Bwire, Garcia's most famous tutor peered at Garcia before finally recognizing him. "What do you want this time?" His cracked and broken voice carried no trace of the once-rich baritone that had often castigated Garcia mercilessly. "Always to me you come when you're in trouble. It is what this time?"

Bwire settled back down in his chair. His apartment was sparse compared to the opulence of Garcia's, but it was the sparseness of a once-sharp mind. There was nothing here that didn't belong, that had no purpose; similarly, nothing was missing.

"I can't stay long." Garcia nervously brushed back his dark hair and sat on the edge of one of the other chairs. He could barely hear the hum of the city outside Bwire's windows.

"I know, I know." Bwire waved a peevish hand. "That old bag won't let anyone stay any longer than a goddamn waver of her goddamn instruments."

The "old bag" to whom Bwire referred was the nurse who had admitted Garcia with the admonition, "You can't stay long. He gets excited and then it's all I can do to keep him from having another attack."

"Sometimes," Bwire said, "I wish they'd just let me die and get it over with."

"Oh, no." Garcia genuinely desired the old man to live. He would miss him deeply.

"Only yourself you think of." Garcia wondered what Bwire was referring to; his attention wandered more and more as he grew older, until sometimes it was impossible to figure out what he was talking about. But sometimes it was just Bwire's oblique way of referring to things. "It is what this time?"

"I wish I knew." He tried to find the words to explain his uneasiness, but there were none. "At the party last night I... well, I couldn't enjoy myself."

"I never cared for parties myself." The old man's voice was sharp and critical, as if to say that parties were pointless and a waste of valuable time.

"But that's the point!" The words burst from Garcia. "I've always enjoyed parties, but this time..."

"You didn't get your usual attention?" A smile played at the edges of Bwire's mouth."

"No, it wasn't that. I just didn't enjoy the attention as much. I felt like... like the third movement of Radcliffe's last sonata."

Bwire raised an eyebrow. The smile was gone from his face. "The one he wrote before committing suicide."

The thought had not occurred to Garcia. "Yes, but I'm not..."

"I know, I know." Bwire shifted in his chair, trying to find a nonexistent comfortable spot. "Do you remember what Radcliffe wrote then?" Garcia shook his head. "'I have tried to find something in music. But it wasn't there. Perhaps it never had been. Perhaps it was just a worm. Without the worm, I would never have done what little I have, like a tiny rosebush in a vast garden. Without the worm, there would have been no roses.'"

"I'm not sure I..."

"So you didn't enjoy your adulation last night?"

"No. There was a woman there..."

Bwire smiled again. "Isn't there *always* a woman there?"

"She... she was very critical of my apartment and she was right, she got me to thinking..."

"So? To think of what?"

"I'm not sure. But I feel as if I've lost touch with my music, that it's become just a means to more adulation, to silly childish belongings, and not an end in itself."

And once it had been. Once Garcia had lived for his music. It had never palled on him, but slowly, insidiously, without his even being aware of its loss, it had been drained away from him.

Bwire leaned back in his chair and closed his eyes. "You are the finest autarist who has ever lived, Garcia." He opened his eyes, fastening them on his former pupil. "I do not say that lightly. But you have so much to learn as a human being."

"But there's so much left to learn as..."

"...as a musician?" The old master leaned forward in his chair. "Who is there for you to learn from? Who is there who can do anything on the autar that you can't?"

"No one," Garcia said softly. "No one I know of."

"Is there anyone who plays faster than you, who has surer touch, who can play any kind of music better than you?" Garcia shook his head. "Where do you go now, Garcia? What do you do now?"

"I don't know." Garcia's voice was a whisper.

"Is there anyone but you who can play that piece that Carter wrote for you?"

"I don't think so."

The old man put his gnarled hands on the arms of his chair and pushed himself up. He walked painfully over to the simple window that looked out over the sunlit city. Outside that window, the impersonal and antiseptic face of the city stared uncaringly at the two musicians. Bwire stared defiantly back at it for a long moment before turning back to Garcia.

"Hard," he said. "It *is* hard." He walked over and placed his hand on Garcia's shoulder. "In many ways, you are my own son and you suffer, I suffer. Your arm, I grieved and hurt too when you lost it."

"I know," Garcia said softly.

"But now it is time for you to grow again and there is no help that I can give. You need to reach outside yourself, Garcia; you need to be more than a performer."

The words meant little to Garcia; they touched no sensitive spot inside him. When he added them to the inchoate roil of his emotions, they clarified nothing.

"What do you suggest?" he asked at last.

"A student, perhaps."

"I'm no teacher."

"You should be, perhaps."

"I couldn't teach anyone. I don't have enough patience."

"I'll contact the conservatory. I'll have them send their best student." Garcia started to protest, but the old man held up his hand. "No. Listen, Garcia. Only to try, that's all I ask of you. To reach beyond yourself, to help someone else." He paused. "Was I so wrong before?" he asked softly.

"No." Garcia remembered how Bwire had helped him find Stella Blue when he was frantically looking for her. But he was uncertain: had he not found her, she might still be alive and he would still have his arm. On the other hand, his music would perhaps still be clinically pure and emotionally dead. Sterile. It seemed nothing ever came for free; nothing of value was ever bought without pain.

Chapter 4

Garcia's first student, a young man named Jorme, was tall and gangling, with large, clumsy, awkward hands. He didn't seem to know what to do with them, and they were in constant motion, pointless movements that had neither beginning nor end. His long oval face was pocked with pimples and had an unattractive marbled appearance. This was the young man whom Bwire had assured Garcia was the most advanced student at the conservatory.

Jorme was carrying one of the most expensive mass-production autars, a GBM 60K, its finish already showing the wear of much use and playing.

"Sit down." Garcia felt nearly as awkward as Jorme appeared to be. "Would you care for some wine?"

"Uh, sure." Jorme sat stiffly on the edge of the least comfortable chair in the room, the one in which Garcia usually sat himself.

"Relax." Garcia poured two glasses of wine. "I'm not sure I'll be able to help you very much. You're the first student I've ever had."

"You are? I mean, I am?" Jorme's hands wandered aimlessly over the autar case. "That's... quite an honor. I mean, being *your* first student."

"It might be something of a disaster." Garcia handed the wine to Jorme. "I don't quite know how to begin." Jorme said nothing, waiting until Garcia started to sip his wine before he did so himself, copying Garcia. "Well, maybe you'd just better play something for me, so I'll know what you can do."

Jorme began with a simple exercise, which he executed flawlessly, despite his obvious nervousness. "I hope you can do something more complex than that," Garcia said sarcastically, surprised to hear in the tone of his voice the same mannerisms Bwire had used with him.

"I just thought I'd... I'd start with something easy and work my way up."

"Keep going." Garcia tried to keep Bwire's wry sarcasm out of his voice, but the effort was unsuccessful.

Jorme went through increasingly more difficult pieces, making occasional nervous mistakes that happened less frequently as he became more absorbed in the music. Technique was not Jorme's strong point; as he began to perform concert pieces, Garcia could see his forte was the fire and drive Garcia's own early performances had lacked. But, though Jorme always played the correct notes, his style lacked the crispness and clarity of Garcia's.

"Here! Wait a minute." Garcia interrupted Jorme's playing. The youngster looked up, his face looking as though he expected to be chastised, a puppy about to be whipped. "Listen to this." Garcia played the last four bars that Jorme had played. "Do you hear the difference?"

"I... I'm not sure."

"Play it again." Jorme played a bar and a half before Garcia stopped him. "Your phrasing is sloppy on that triplet. Listen." Garcia played it again. "Do you see?"

"I think so." Jorme was hesitant.

For the next half hour they continued in that vein, Garcia trying to correct Jorme's lack of clarity. It was very frustrating: it was so clear and obvious what was wrong, but he had trouble finding the words to explain it. Frequently Jorme claimed he couldn't see any difference and, when he did, he was unable to correct himself. He even argued once that his own version was better. Only one time was he able to duplicate Garcia's performance.

When Jorme at last was gone, Garcia felt drained. It was far more exhausting than a concert! It forced him to question his own biases and the techniques that had become second nature to him. Explaining to someone else what he did was far more difficult than actually doing it.

But there was a feeling of exultation in the experience as well, not as profound as that he had once known as a performer, but a strong echo of that feeling, and he welcomed it. Perhaps there *was* more, after all. Still, he didn't feel teaching would ever be as fulfilling and important to him as actually making the music himself.

Restless and excited, he took an electrocab down to his agent's office to talk about his upcoming concert tour. When he mentioned he had taken on a student, Renard frowned. "I don't like it," he said. "This is going to interfere with your concentration. It's going to be a drain on your energies."

Garcia watched Renard's secretary, who was querying the computer terminal. "I don't think so," he said. "It might even help me."

"How could it?"

"It's making me think more about what I'm doing, making me more aware of what's going on when I play the autar."

"And you think that's good?"

"Isn't it?"

"You ever heard about the centipede who started to think about which leg went first and fell flat on its face?"

Garcia stifled the urge to argue. "That could happen, I guess. But if it does, I'll just have to quit teaching, that's all. Don't worry about it."

"Yeah, yeah. By the time you realize what's happening, it'll already be too late. You'll be thinking too much."

"Don't worry about it." Garcia punched Renard lightly and playfully on the shoulder. "You've already made your bundle off me. And, hell, I'll still know what I'm doing. It won't work that way, believe me, Renard."

"Sure, sure."

"By the way, what happened to that girl you brought to my party the other night?"

"Shaara?"

"Yeah. What do you know about her?"

"Interested?"

"A little."

"Forget it. She's not your type."

"Afraid I'll steal her from you?"

Renard smiled. "Not at all. She's too rich for my blood. Totally out of my class. There's nothing between us and there never will be."

"Then what were you doing with her?"

"She wanted to meet you. And it doesn't hurt to indulge the rich. You're a hot item, you know."

"So you keep telling me."

Renard's secretary turned to the two men. "Everything's ready now, sir."

"Thanks, Lyana. Let's talked a look at what I've lined up for your next concert series." Renard pressed the button on the display unit on his desk. "Incidentally, Shaara would like you to come to a party her father's giving next week."

"What?" Garcia couldn't stifle the grin that arose at his agent's non sequiturs and self-contradictions.

"You heard me. She'll send a chauffeur for you. Enjoy it. Now... your tour starts two weeks from tomorrow right here in town. We've got just enough time to advertise what you're going to perform. Have you decided yet?"

Chapter 5

Mars Ruby ran her nails lightly over the coarse, dark hair of Garcia's chest. "You're putting on weight."

"I know. I can't seem to help it."

"You're going to get fat." Garcia grimaced. "What's this?"

"What's what?"

"Oh, isn't that cute?" She smiled coquettishly at him.

"What is it?" he asked in irritation, sitting up to see what she was looking at.

"See it? Right there." She pulled a small tuft of hair straight out. "It's a white hair. You're growing old, too, Garcia."

"Is that all?" Garcia lay back again, disgruntled.

"Old and fat. Soon you'll be old and fat. What will you do then?"

"Will you quit making such a big thing out of it?"

"My, aren't you the irritable one today. What's bothering you?"

"Nothing's bothering me. Nothing but you."

"Garcia?" Her voice took on a placating, querulous tone. "It isn't going to help if you keep it inside you. What's wrong?"

She ran her hand gently through his curly black hair. He wondered if she was seeing gray strands there as well.

"I'm not sure."

"Are you in love?"

"Don't be silly. Of course not."

"What about that girl at your party? What was her name? Shaara?"

"Give me credit for *some* brains."

"Love has nothing to do with brains. Look at Justin and *his* wife."

"He loves her."

"Yes, of course he does. But he could do so much better."

"She's a damn good musician."

"And I'm a damn good lover. Do you love me?"

"Of course." Garcia pulled her close to him but, after a short moment of acquiescence, she pulled away.

"But you're not in love with me."

"What's the difference?"

"There's a big difference." She shook her head and her long red hair tossed around on her back. "Do you want to marry me?"

Garcia thought for a moment, trying to find a way to tell the truth without hurting Ruby's feelings.

"Forget it. It's obvious you don't. Don't worry about it. I like you a lot, Garcia, but I wouldn't want to spend the rest of my life with you."

"Oh." Garcia was slightly disturbed by her statement. He moved toward the edge of the bed.

"Now *I've* hurt *you*."

"No, you haven't. Really."

She sighed and moved to his side, caressing his back. "You're so mixed up, Garcia. I wish I knew what was wrong. I wish I knew how to help you."

"Bwire thinks being a teacher will help."

"It doesn't?"

Garcia shook his head slowly. "No. I enjoy it more than I thought I would. Jorme's a nice kid, and I think we're going to be friends."

"Good. You need another friend."

He turned to face her. "But it's not enough. There's something... I don't know, like something missing. Teaching fills it a little bit, but not enough."

"Performing isn't enough?"

"It doesn't seem to be. Not anymore." How could he explain it to her? He had come to the end of the road of his development as an autarist, and there were no challenges left, no new roads to conquer.

He dimmed the already faint light in the room.

"Maybe you ought to try something else. Like another instrument." Garcia made a gruff disparaging sound in his throat. "You ought to see Gang's Fool."

"Another of your popular groups?"

"Cotton Jennie's body is so in tune with her computer, it's just incredibly smooth, and Amis plays rhythms on his percusser that are almost as complex as *grilly*."

"But there's no feedback to those systems."

"Sure there is. They don't use if it often, but it's there."

Garcia sighed. "I don't mean electronic feedback."

"What are you talking about then?"

"The feedback a performer gets from his instrument. The tension of the strings, the way they respond under his fingers. You don't get that kind of feedback from completely computerized music, and so you can't get the nuances, the subtleties. Do you know what I mean?"

Mars Ruby moved under the covers, trying to find a comfortable position. "I don't think you *want* to listen to them. Your mind is closed."

He stared at the stars on his ceiling, moving imperceptibly and as surely as the ones in the sky, and exactly in tune with them. Was she right, or was it her mind that was closed? He didn't know the answer.

"Let's get some sleep." His hands moved briefly over the bed's controls and the cool spring breeze of a long-forgotten New England evening played gently over their bodies.

Chapter 6

"Ready to call it quits?"

"Yeah." Jorme laid his autar down and wiped his forehead with the back of his forearm. "That was rough."

"It sure was." Garcia's voice was sardonic.

"I really don't see why you think it's so important, though. So what if it isn't quite as clean and sharp as it could be? Only half a dozen people'll know the difference."

"*You'll* know." Garcia brushed back a lock of his dark hair.

"So what?"

"Look at it this way, Jorme." Garcia poured some wine. "Sure, no one else knows the difference... now. But being *able* to it, well, that gives you so much freedom, so many more options when you perform. And, when you record, your recorded performance is going to last a hell of a lot longer if your attack is clean and sharp."

"What are you getting at?"

"Maybe only half a dozen people know the difference now. But then years from now it'll be half a hundred. And then more, and more. And something else will be on the outside edges of technique, where only half a dozen people can appreciate it. And, who knows? Maybe *you'll* be the guy who comes up with it."

"Yeah." Jorme grinned. "Wouldn't that be something." He took the glass from Garcia and began drinking, more confidently than before.

"I'm sure you will. You've got the ability."

"You really think so?" Jorme looked at his hands. "Sometimes I wonder. Did you ever wonder whether you'd make it?"

Garcia smiled. "No. I guess I always knew I would. It was just a matter of time. I got pretty impatient sometimes, though."

"I wish I could be that certain. I mean, everybody says I'm good. You're not the first, but it really means quite a lot coming from you, you know?"

"You wouldn't be here if a lot of people didn't think you were damn good. I don't have time to waste on amateurs."

"But I'm scared. I mean, with all the performances I've given at schools and things, you'd think I wouldn't get stage fright. But the thought of really going out on my own and giving my *own* performance, not just one with a lot of students, it scares me."

"There's nothing to be scared of." It was one more thing about Jorme that Garcia couldn't comprehend: he himself had always been a performer; it was what he lived for. It was the loss of that edge that now distressed him.

"I know, I know." Jorme began pacing the room. "A lot of the other students feel that way. About half of them have already given solo concerts. I'm just about the only who hasn't who's near the top of things."

"You're not near the top. You're *at* the top."

"You think so? You really think so?"

"Of course. You're the top student at the school. That's why you're here." It was incomprehensible that Jorme could have come so far without having had a solo concert. They were so completely different from each other, coming at the same thing from completely different angles. And yet... Jorme had talent and lots of it. If he only had the confidence to go with it, he would be unbeatable. Garcia sat down in the chair that Jorme had vacated. "And it's time you had a solo concert of your own."

"I don't think I'm quite ready."

"You'll never be quite ready. You're good, damn good, Jorme, and it's time you went out on your own. I'm going to talk to Renard and see if he'll take you on as a client. Do you mind?"

"Well... no. But I don't think he likes me."

Garcia smiled. "It has nothing to do with you. He just doesn't like the idea of me teaching anybody. He thinks I'll lose my touch if I have to analyze what I'm doing. He forgets that all my technique and craft are based on a very thorough analysis of the autar and what it can do."

"I'm still not sure it's a good idea."

"Wait a minute!" Garcia rose suddenly from the chair, facing Jorme, his eyes twinkling. "I've got an idea. We can perform together. You and me. That way I can keep teaching you. What a promotional stunt. Garcia and his first student. His first protégé. Hey! What do you think?"

"I think it's scary."

"I'm sure Renard will go for it."

Garcia asked the supervisor for a line to his agent, eager to share the idea with Renard. But after he had outlined the entire idea, Renard said, "I think it's dumb."

"But you'll do it?"

"Do I have any choice?"

Garcia regarded the ceiling in a studied pose of contemplation. "I could go to work at the conservatory as a teacher."

"I'll think about it."

Garcia closed the connection and turned to Jorme, who was frowning. "Don't worry about it. He'll come around."

Chapter 7

The cranky, crotchety Bwire whom Garcia was used to, even fond of, was gone, replaced by a more introspective and reminiscing Bwire. He sat in his chair, seeming to have shrunk even in the short time since Garcia had last seen him. "So, you and Jorme will share concerts? A good move. Grow, Garcia, grow. Stagnate, and you die. Inside, a piece of you dies. Enough pieces die, and what are you? A technician, a craftsman, yes, but not human. Not really human."

"Of course," Garcia said politely.

"This is a good thing for you. Like Stella Blue. It will be hard, yes, that I know, but it must be done. Don't ever doubt it, Garcia. Don't ever doubt it." The old man reached out and gripped Garcia's real arm, gripping it tightly, almost painfully, a claw, a talon, ripping into Garcia's flesh. At first Garcia recoiled at the touch from this ancient flesh but he caught that move before it had barely begun, relaxed, and covered Bwire's hands with his own. And in that simple act, he remembered the supple and flexible fingers that had taught him so much of what he knew about the autar; he looked briefly into his own future, seeing his own fingers grow gnarled and knotty. But on one hand they would remain smooth and supple, capable. Or would his nerves decay also, so that he would lose control of even of his artificial arm?

"Play for me, Garcia. Play for an old man."

"I didn't bring my autar with me. I'm sorry. I really am." And he was. It had been a long time since he had played for the old master.

But Bwire only smiled. "Really, Garcia, you don't think that I would be without an autar, do you? Even now?" Bwire's voice caught briefly but, when he spoke again, after a very brief pause, there was no edge of emotion to it. "Over there. To your left." As he spoke, he pressed buttons on his chair and a cabinet that had been opaque grew transparent; its top slowly tilted back to reveal the venerable autar that Bwire had often played for Garcia.

"But... I couldn't..."

"Please," the old man whispered. "It was meant to be played and it will be yours one day."

Garcia carefully picked up the instrument. It had been handmade by Althor Burn, the same craftsman who had made two of his own concert instruments, but this one had been made thirty years earlier, when Althor Burn was just making a reputation for himself. It was simpler, less versatile, but Garcia was used to that, having played the ancient instrument that had reputedly belonged to Radcliffe. Such instruments demanded more from the performer than the more complex modern ones. But this was Bwire's instrument and, as such, it meant even more to Garcia.

He powered the instrument and began playing, softly, delicately, starting with simple computer harmonies, shifting keys fluently, while Bwire sat with his eyes smiling. Garcia played the music of Radcliffe and of Scheiner, of Thomas the Rhymer, and of Mooncat. He played his own transcription of one of Stella Blue's songs, the computer playing a sitaresque wailing behind his own raw strumming, simple but powerful. And finally he played some of Bwire's own compositions, impishly sneaking in one of the exercises Bwire originally had given him.

The old master opened his eyes. "Very nice, Garcia. You know, five years ago, that was something you wouldn't have done."

Garcia nodded. "It wouldn't even have occurred to me."

"And where will you be when you return, I wonder? What will you be like? I will be very curious to find out. It will be worth living for." He rose very wearily from his chair and walked over to Garcia. The old, once-agile claw gripped Garcia's shoulder. "Come back as soon as possible, Garcia."

"I will." His voice was almost a whisper. "As soon as I can."

Chapter 8

Shaara agreed to let Garcia bring Jorme to the party and the young autarist was at Garcia's apartment long before Muenstretiger's chauffeur arrived. He was dressed in ill-fitting brand-new garments, and was just as nervous as he had been when he had arrived for his first lesson, if not more so.

"Do I look all right?" he asked Garcia.

"You look fine." There was no sense in telling Jorme how he really appeared.

"I'm so afraid I'll make a fool of myself. I've never been to a place like this before."

"If it'll make you feel any better, neither have I."

"How can you be so calm?"

Garcia shrugged. "What else is there to do?" How could he possibly explain to Jorme? Even if Garcia had never been a party at the estate of someone as rich and powerful as Muenstretiger, he had been to enough parties held by some of the more influential people in the city, and they were all the same: a bore.

When the chauffeur at last arrived, Jorme had already gulped down two glasses of wine so his nervousness had abated somewhat. Muenstretiger's own private vehicle purred electrically through the streets until they reached the estate. It was ringed by a high stone wall with barbed wire at the top. The vehicle stopped at a massive gate that finally swung open on ponderous hinges.

They rode along a long graveled driveway through a park-like expanse to a large mansion that was in perfect condition. Stately trees lined the roadway, but a large spacious lawn surrounded the house.

"They're really cautious about intruders, aren't they?" Jorme said.

"Wouldn't you be?"

A liveried butler, not a robot, greeted them and led them to a large hall, full of people milling about, and announced them even as Shaara and her father were coming toward them. Muenstretiger moved swiftly and surely, like a wolf set loose in a sheepfold. His full head of hair was completely white but the eyebrows were still dark. He took Garcia's hand in a grip that was firm yet not too firm. "I'm pleased to meet you, Garcia. I've enjoyed listening to you play, and it's a pleasure to meet you in person." His voice was rich and full, without being overly loud. It was the voice of a man with power and money, a man who was certain of himself, a man who needed no ostentation to feel secure. Garcia had never had to worry about money in his entire life, but he was a pauper compared to this man.

He muttered the usual inane social amenities then introduced Jorme.

"Yes, your student. Well, I've never heard you play, young man, but I'm sure you must be most accomplished. I look forward to hearing you some day."

Jorme stuttered out his thanks.

"Shaara, why don't you take them over to the bar?"

She had been silent during the greetings, but Garcia kept meeting her eyes, seeing a small quiet smile on her face. It was hard to say anything to her while her father was there. In the gaudy company of the party, she seemed drab and unspectacular. Her face was sharp and angular; her nose was crooked, and her hair was cut severely short. Garcia had always been enamored of long hair. Everything about her was wrong and nothing was right. She was short and slim, her figure more boyish than womanly; her breasts were small bumps, not the ripe and pendulant fruits of some of the more generously-endowed women at the party. Her shimmering blouse was closed at the throat, and her short skirt revealed her shapely legs without revealing anything else.

But when she smiled at Garcia, he found himself with a lump in his throat. For a moment he was an awkward schoolboy, a coltish acned fifteen, his veneer of worldliness and suaveness ripped away.

"It's good to see you again," he said quietly, with a warmth to his voice that didn't betray the turmoil within.

"It's good to see you again, too. And I'm pleased to meet you, Jorme. I look forward to hearing you perform sometime."

Jorme's head bobbed awkwardly. "Thank you."

Garcia chose a wine from the bar, and Jorme followed suit.

"That's an excellent year," Shaara said approvingly. "You have good taste, Garcia."

"Surprised?"

"A little."

"I happen to appreciate the good things, Shaara, though I may not be exactly in your league."

She laughed. "When you reach a certain point, Garcia, there's not much difference, no matter how much higher you go. You're quite close to that point."

He wondered if she were toying with him, slumming, as it were, playing with a well-known musician. Was he just to be the latest conquest in a long string that, perhaps, included an artist, an actor, a politician, and Lord knows was else?

The room was filled with colorful people, attractive women and impressive men. A noble and elderly lady walked by, her skin still young although her hair was white. "Ah, you're Garcia." She took his hand very gently. "I've enjoyed your music *so* much."

On the far side of the room a woman in blue fur walked regally. Her belly was flat and sleek, covered with pale blue soft fur that blended gently with the glistening blue fur of her pubic area, while her legs and back were fully furred with the same color. A tail, long and somewhat prehensile, protruded from her back and twitched about merrily. She delighted in tapping people on the shoulder from behind with it as she talked to them. Her breasts were firm and pale under the downy fur of her front, and her ears were slightly pointed. She wore no clothing whatsoever and Garcia knew that the soles of her feet would be heavily padded. She would have to be quite rich to afford such an operation: it was costly both in time and money. The alterations were more than skin deep.

He knew all too well the expense of such surgery. He touched his right arm. It was far less expensive than the surgery the blue-furred woman had undergone. And not much less than that which kept the white-haired woman's face young. He wondered why she didn't dye her hair. But then, perhaps, she would lose much of her regal mien. There were so many options available, options that pushed back the boundaries of aging. It wouldn't be long before the average man or woman lived a full and viable life past the age of one hundred. Many of the rich and powerful already did so.

Shaara introduced the two musicians to members of the richest and most prestigious families in the country, people who wielded power as though it were their own personal prerogative, without thought or consideration. Most of them seemed delighted to meet him and disappointed that he had not brought his autar with him. He realized that, although his name and face were better known and more easily recognized than any of theirs, it was they who had the real control of things. He was merely a plaything to them, a toy, a pawn, a court jester, a pet monkey, a prize to display as they would a painting by an old master or a sculpture or a rare recording or a fine wine.

The young scion of the Mont'Illiano family was in his late twenties but reputedly was already in control of most of the communications net, as his father slowly removed himself from the family business.

"Garcia! A pleasure. I've enjoyed your music." Mont'Illiano's interest seemed genuine, his smile a warm one without any falseness. "I hope to see you here often. Enjoying yourself?"

"Yes, thank you," Garcia said politely, still unsure of himself in this different stratum of society, feeling his way along slowly.

"Good. We need someone here besides all these stodgy old birds without any talent except for making money."

"Monty!" Shaara admonished him.

"Well, it's true. Look at me. I can talk the birds out of the trees sometimes, especially at board meetings but, other than that, I'm useless."

Why was Shaara interested in Garcia rather than in this brash young man with whom she had so much more in common? They were both drawn from the same mold. Social parasites? Perhaps. That was the cloak they both drew over themselves, but Garcia saw something further under the surface. He had heard Mont'Illiano referred to as a bloodsucker, a leech, and it was true that he took much out of the system for his own use. Nonetheless, he put much back in. A parasite? No. A social symbiont. It would all die and wither without Mont'Illiano and his compatriots, and Garcia would die and wither with it.

The leader of the Tibaldo clan, rulers of the electromotive industry, was also young, a man in his early forties, his full head of dark hair laced with gray, steel in his smile. His gray-blue eyes seemed to pierce Garcia, taking his measure in a few swift seconds.

He moved quickly through the social amenities, and said, "This student of yours, Jorme. Is he good?" As Garcia and Shaara moved through the party, Jorme had left them, drawn into conversation with some younger people.

"He's quite good. You'll be hearing his name frequently very soon."

"I hope so. We need more fine musicians. You knew Bwire, didn't you?"

"I learned a great deal from him." Garcia was surprised that Tibaldo knew of Bwire, who had retired from performing more than twenty years earlier and had been out of the public eye for nearly as long.

"Artists such as yourself and Bwire are rare; you're national treasures and should be treated as such."

"Put in dusty cabinets and taken out on holidays?" Garcia had tried to make the tone of his voice light but a trace of bitterness surfaced in it nonetheless.

Tibaldo looked at him sharply. "No, that's not what I meant. But it *is* true that you should learn to pace yourself and not burn yourself out while you're still young. You've got a long life ahead of you, probably even longer than you think. There's a lot of interesting things happening in medicine and areas like that. Get Muenstretiger to tell you about them sometime."

Jorme was flushed with excitement when he returned to Garcia's side. "This is one hell of a party! Do you know who I was talking to just a few minutes ago?"

"No." Garcia knew very well whom Jorme had been talking to.

"Pentland LaCroix!"

"The HV star?" Pentland LaCroix was the current sex symbol of the solar system.

Jorme nodded, wide-eyed.

"What did she say to you?"

"What didn't she say to me? She's something else." Jorme shook his head in wonderment. He lowered his voice. "Frankly, I think she'd like to go to bed with you."

Garcia smiled. "Well, you tell her that you have to check out all my bedmates personally first. That you're my official bedmate checker."

Jorme smiled bashfully. "I couldn't do that."

Garcia put a fatherly hand on Jorme's shoulder. It seemed so strange that this awkward, shy young man could be so at home and so skillful on the autar.

He toyed with the idea of moving in on either the blue-furred woman or Pentland LaCroix. No, he thought, not Pentland. He would leave her for Jorme.

"Garcia! I heard you were here but I couldn't believe it." The man was vaguely familiar, as were so many of the people he had already met. But this man didn't have that now-familiar air of authority and power; instead there was something foppish about him. His clothes were those of a dandy: they were too neatly creased and folded, too sharp and meticulous. His face was chiseled out of granite: a nose too perfect in its angularity, a chin perfectly noble, a mouth perfectly proportioned, and steel-blue eyes. Nonetheless, there was a softness to the face and a puffiness that underlay the features, already beginning to show their age. "You don't recognize me, do you?"

"No, I'm afraid not."

The other seemed delighted. "How perfect. How absolutely perfect. Practically everyone in the world knows me and recognizes me, even the powerful people in this very room, perhaps they especially, but the one person in the world whom I admire most fails to recognize me."

"I feel I *should* recognize you but I can't quite place you."

"Jack Orion."

"Of course. I'm sorry. I should have…"

"No apologies, please." Orion held his hands up in an attempt to stop Garcia's apology. "I am delighted."

Perhaps Jack Orion exaggerated a bit in saying everyone in the world would recognize him, but it wasn't a large exaggeration. He was one of the most popular commentators in the world, his sharp commentary feared by those in the public eye, from the president of the world council to the lowliest entertainer, and enjoyed by the public, especially the *barraquistes*. He had a reputation as a muckraker and none of Garcia's friends had much use for him, or much good to say about him.

"I've admired you for years." Orion took Garcia by the elbow and led him toward the bar. "You've become quite a legend down in the *barraque*."

"Legends are supposed to be dead," Garcia growled, not knowing how to get away from this effusive parasite.

Orion laughed. "Well, no one thinks you're dead. In fact, there's a… a rumor, I guess you'd call it, or a prediction that, when you return to the *barraque*, you'll lead the *barraquistes* in a revolt."

Garcia tried to echo Orion's laugh but it was forced and unreal. "Well, there's little chance of that."

"Well, I see you two have met." Mont'Illiano came up from behind them. "May the better man win." He had his arms around them both, like a referee between two fighters at the beginning of a match

"It's not like that at all, Monty," Orion said. "We're not competitors. We walk in two different worlds."

"There are many levels of competition." Mont'Illiano punched them both lightly on the shoulder, and Orion's face darkened. "Good luck to both of you. Or whatever."

"What was he talking about?" Garcia asked as the young man walked away.

"Who knows?" Orion muttered angrily. "I don't like that man, Garcia."

"Isn't he your boss, in a way?"

"Yes. He runs the communications networks and I work for them so I guess you could say that. But that doesn't mean I have to like them. He toys with people, Garcia; he tries to stir up trouble between them just so he can watch it. He has no respect for other people."

"He seems all right to me."

"Just wait. And watch him. This is the first time you've met him, right? The first time you've been to Muenstretiger's or any of their places?"

"Yes."

"Well, I've been with them for two years now. Ever since I got my own show. They think they're keeping an eye on me this way, but that works two ways: I'm also keeping an eye on *them,* and I'll be ready for them when the time comes. I suppose..." Orion thought better of whatever he was going to say. Garcia waited while the commentator took a stiff drink from his whiskey. "You know, I'm responsible for your being here tonight."

"You are?" Garcia raised an eyebrow.

Orion nodded. "I was the one who introduced Shaara to your recordings. She'd never even heard of you before that. Can you imagine?"

Garcia smiled. "There are plenty of people who have never heard of me."

"Maybe, maybe not. But the important people have. Other musicians, people who appreciate good music. And you're kind of a hero to the *barraquistes*, even though you've never been one of them. That incident a couple of years ago, the girl..."

"Stella Blue."

"Yes. Well, they say you've become one of them, in heart, and there are songs about you and her."

"How do you know all this?"

"It's my business. I've got contacts everywhere."

"Are you boring Garcia?" Shaara rejoined them.

"No, I'm just..."

"Hush." She stretched up and kissed him briefly, then took both men by the arm. "Stop being so silly."

"He wasn't boring me, Shaara."

"I don't want to hear about it. This is a party and I don't want the two of you fighting. Will you dance with me, Garcia?"

"I'm afraid I don't dance."

"How depressing. Well, you won't mind if Jack and I do, will you?"

"Not at all. Go ahead."

She danced away in Jack Orion's arms, laughing.

"She's a strong-willed girl," a rich baritone voice said behind Garcia. It was Muenstretiger. "I really don't know how to control her." He sighed, and it seemed incongruous that such a self-controlled man should sigh. "I'm glad you're here, Garcia." He placed his hand on Garcia's shoulder. "I'm glad she likes your music. That's one thing at least that Jack Orion has done for her. She'd never heard of you before, but you're all she talks about now. You're good. Almost as good as Bwire." Garcia wondered at the softness that stole over Muenstretiger's face, replacing the steel, and the far-off expression in his eyes.

Chapter 9

The party started to break up as couples and groups began to move toward the door. "I guess I'd better be leaving," Garcia said to Shaara. "Have you seen Jorme lately?"

"Oh, the night's still young, Garcia. A bunch of us are going to The Welcome Machine. Surely you'll come along?"

"I don't know, I..."

"Don't be one of the old folks." Mont'Illiano slipped up behind them. "We're going to do the town. Besides, I haven't had time for a good talk with you. Be a good chap."

"I don't know. If Jorme..."

"I've already talked to him and it's all set. All five of us will take one car, and there'll be others. Even Jack Orion." Mont'Illiano winked at Garcia. "So you see there's going to be lots of fun."

Jorme and the lovely Pentland LaCroix came up then, Jorme's face flushed, whether with alcohol, excitement, or emotion, Garcia couldn't say. Probably all three. "Are you going to come with us, Garcia? Please do. It sounds like lots of fun."

"All right, all right."

"Excellent. Shaara, you get the limousine ready and I'll round up the others." Mont'Illiano moved off briskly, looking about eagerly for the other members of their party.

The entryway to The Welcome Machine was a gigantic metal maw, studded with teeth that reminded Garcia all too well of the river cleaner that had stolen his flesh-and-blood arm from him. He could hear the steady thrum and clanking of machinery behind the walls of the narrow passageway. The corridor ended on a metal mesh catwalk overlooking a cavernous room where students, artists and pseudo-artists talked, flirted, danced, drank, and occasionally listened to the music at the far end of the room.

As usual in the post-midnight hour, The Welcome Machine was full. A waiter, dressed as a robot, but in reality probably a student at the conservatory trying to make ends meet, approached. "Five?" he asked in a tinny voice.

"There's more of us coming," Shaara said. "About twenty, all told." The robot/waiter executed a neat mechanical turn and led them to a group of tables halfway through the room.

Garcia was totally out of his element. He simply wasn't used to being surrounded by people he didn't know, strangers in grotesque costumes and eerie styles. A man walked by whose face was entirely covered by hair, only his surprisingly placid blue eyes visible, a very minor version of the type of operation the blue-furred woman had taken. Many of The Welcome Machine's customers had had minor operations of that sort—a gold-plated mechanical finger, oddly-shaped ears, small patches of various-colored fur. None of the café's ordinary patrons could afford a major operation, but many of them sported whatever they could afford, in an effort to proclaim their individuality.

Others, unwilling to undergo such operations for whatever reasons—lack of money or fear of undertaking something so implacably permanent—wore their hair in strange shapes, shaved their heads in erotic patterns, wore eye-jewelry and exotic clothing. Some of the women sported creatures that had been bred and created as pets, wide-eyed, fluffy mammals that scurried in and out of billowing sleeves and bouffant hairdos, staring out in fear and curiosity.

They were, thought Garcia, proclaiming themselves talented, when indeed they had no talent. It was the handful of unornamented, unmodified humans scattered throughout the club who probably were the most talented. The large man with the full red beard at a nearby table, for example, looking for all the world as countless generations of artists had looked. Was he a sculptor perhaps, who could make a bust of Shaara that would be absolutely lifelike, then turn around and do a completely incomprehensible abstract mobile? Perhaps a scriptor for holovision or a director. Not likely to be an actor, not with such a full beard, or even a musician. A musician might settle for a small beard or a mustache, but a beard that full might get in the way.

The fake-robot waiter took their orders, stood at the table a long moment, then opened the panel in his chest and delivered their drinks to them, just like an ordinary robot waiter. Garcia wondered briefly how the trick was done. Then it turned smartly in a smooth toe-heel step and moved mechanically to another table.

"Well, this wasn't quite what I had expected," Shaara said.

"What did you expect?" Garcia asked.

"I'm not sure. Something more... more earthy, I guess, more decadent."

Garcia smiled. "According to everything I've heard, all the decadence is mired in the, uh, the ruling classes."

Shaara scowled. "I've always wondered what the... the simple folk do for amusement."

"This isn't exactly the simple folk, Shaara. For that, you need to go down to the *barraque*. And that's something I wouldn't suggest you do."

"Why not? You used to go there, didn't you?"

"Yes." Garcia's voice was soft, barely audible. "Years ago. And then, only for a short time."

"And what do they do down there for enjoyment?"

"They kill themselves. Slowly, with drugs or drink, or quickly, with violence."

"I don't believe that. You're exaggerating."

"Perhaps a little. But it's no place for a lady like you. I'd stay away from there, if I were you. This is excitement enough for you."

"This," she said very emphatically, "is boring." There was an edge of irritation and annoyance to her voice.

Like the waiters, the musicians were dressed as robots, moving in syncopated rhythms. It was a watered-down version of the *grilly* music that was very popular in the *barraque*, a discordant music with disturbing rhythms that was very difficult for a non-*barraquiste* to master. The band on the stage of The Welcome Machine was stiff, though perhaps no one in the club knew it but Garcia, who had spent several months living in the *barraque* after the death of Stella Blue. The keyboardist lacked the pedal dexterity so important to a *grilly* keyboardist. His bass was a simple programmed thrumming, without the constantly changing rhythms of the skilled tuntong player. The autar player was, of course, no more than adequate. Garcia wondered if he was a student at the conservatory. His instrument was a quarter tone out of key.

The one saving grace of the group was its singer, a woman with extraordinary range and purity, yet with the ability to growl her notes with appropriate grittiness when the occasion required. It was that very purity, however, that rendered her performance metallic, yes, and robotic, lacking the essence of *grilly* while attempting to elevate it beyond its basic origins.

Shaara noticed Garcia's attention to the music. "Do you know the autar player?"

Garcia shook his head. "I know none of them. The autarist isn't very good, but the singer is quite talented."

"I wonder what she looks like under all that metal."

The trio ended to perfunctory applause; more than half of the audience had been more involved with their own conversations than with the music. Their place was taken by a rather plain-looking woman who danced to recorded music while she slowly took off her garments. Why, Garcia wondered, should that be more erotic than the blue-furred woman, who openly walked about naked. Only when most of her clothes were off did Garcia realize that the woman had a mane of bright red fur that ran down the ridge of her spine to culminate in a short barbed tail. He grinned as soon as he saw the tail and Shaara took him to task for it.

"Really, Garcia, I should think you would get no enjoyment out of such childish activities."

"Once upon a time, Shaara, you would have been right. But I think it's rather cute. She should have horns and a pitchfork, however."

"That would be carrying it too far," Mont'Illiano said.

The evening continued with amateur musicians, a violinist and a guitarist playing Harrigan's Sonata for Guitar and Violin being the most accomplished. Many of the others played the computerized instruments controlled by keyboards and switches that Mars Ruby enjoyed so much.

"Where's Jack Orion?" Garcia asked. "I thought he was going to be here."

Mont'Illiano's grin was mischievous. "I, ah, gave him some misdirections, I'm afraid. He's gone somewhere else, to the Mink Julep, perhaps. I also dropped some hints that we might be going to the *barraque*."

"Oh, Monty, that's a great idea," Shaara said. "Let's go."

"I was just trying to get rid of Orion for a while. He's fun in small doses, but he does get wearisome after a while. Besides, I wanted to talk to Garcia without his distraction."

"You mean we're not going to the *barraque*?" Shaara seemed quite displeased with the thought.

"I don't think that would be a good idea."

"I'm surprised that you allow Orion to run his commentaries on HV," Garcia said. "They seem to be quite contemptuous and critical of a lot of things I should think you'd be interested in keeping as they are."

"Maintaining the status quo," Mont'Illiano said, still smiling. "But you see, Garcia, that's exactly what we're doing."

"I'm afraid I *don't* see."

"Look, if it wasn't Orion, it'd be somebody else. But we can control *him*."

Garcia frowned. "You mean you've bought him? He sure puts on a good act."

Mont'Illiano shook his head, maintaining the grin which was beginning to irritate Garcia. "No, we're more subtle than that. What we do is feed him misinformation, not much, but a little, enough, like I did tonight to keep him away from here, and that keeps him in control, in line. We're not stupid, Garcia."

"If you're not stupid, what are you doing telling *me* all this?"

"Because, Garcia, you're one of us." As Garcia started to protest, Mont'Illiano held up his hands. "Oh, I know *you* don't think so, but you are, or you will be. You'll realize that soon enough. Are you going to tell Orion about this?" Garcia shook his head. "You see?"

ഔ ◁▷ ഏ

It was near dawn when they finally left The Welcome Machine, although the club was still more than half full and it didn't seem as if things were about to wind down. The club wouldn't shut its doors until near noon, the last of its patrons and performers struggling out from the dark recesses into the blinding light of daytime like babies leaving the womb, lost and needing only a slap to begin crying. It wouldn't open again until shortly before midnight.

Mont'Illiano offered them a ride home in his limousine but Shaara refused, insisting that she and Garcia take an electrocab, saying, "I wanted to be alone with you for a while. We haven't had a chance to be alone all night long."

Garcia smiled. "We never have." She smiled back warmly.

"Destination please?" the voice of the driver asked through its speaker.

Garcia looked at Shaara. "What's your address?" Having taken a limousine to her estate, he had no idea what its address was.

"Do you really wish to get rid of me that easily?"

"No."

Their mutual gaze was broken when the driver repeated its question. Garcia gave the address of his apartment.

Chapter 10

A little before noon, although the stars still wheeled sunless overhead on Garcia's ceiling, his supervisor called his name. Garcia grumbled something and nosed back into the warmth of his bed.

"Garcia, I have Mr. Renard waiting to talk to you."

Garcia mumbled something else incomprehensible then said in a sleep-thickened voice, "Renard? What the hell do you want?"

Renard's crisp voice, clean and unwary, replaced the supervisor's. "I've been in touch with Muenstretiger and he wants to see you this afternoon. Will three be convenient?" There was a slight edge of sarcasm to Renard's voice.

"Three? What time is it now?"

"Eleven thirty-two," the supervisor said.

"Three's okay, I guess." He looked at Shaara to confirm it, but she still had her eyes shut, although he suspected she was awake.

"He'll send a limousine over for you at three then," Renard said.

"Fine. Supe?"

"Present," the supervisor said.

"Wake me at two, will you?"

"Programmed."

Garcia turned on his side and tried to find the comfortable abyss of sleep again, not noticing that Shaara's eyes were now open and looking at him a strange knowing expression.

෨◄►෨

When the supervisor woke him at two, the aroma of fresh coffee filled the room, mixed with that of hot buttered toast. Shaara was no longer in bed, but he could hear the sound of water in the convenience. Then the door slid open and she came out, partially dressed, and slapped him on a naked thigh. "Hurry up, or everything will be cold!"

"Don't be silly. Those are canned smells. When will breakfast be ready, supe?"

"I can have juice and coffee for the young lady immediately, if she wants it. Your breakfast will be ready in ten minutes, as usual."

"What do you want for breakfast, Shaara?"

"What are *you* having?"

"Steak and eggs."

"Sounds wonderful. I'll have the same."

"How would you like your steak, ma'am?" the supervisor asked.

"Well done." Garcia looked at her with disappointment.

"And your eggs?"

"Let me have Eggs Martian."

Garcia got off the bed, feeling the aches in his joints beginning to fade away. He had a brisk shower before breakfast.

"Your juice and coffee are ready, ma'am," he heard the supervisor say.

"Shaara," she said firmly.

"Programmed."

≫❮❯≪

The liveried butler again met them at the mansion and led Garcia to a large study while Shaara went up the large stairway that led to the second floor.

Garcia walked around the room, looking at the bookcases. He had seen only a handful of actual books in his life and he reflected there might be more books in this room than there were on the rest of the planet.

He turned at the faint sound of a door opening on the other side of the room.

"Garcia. Glad you could come." Muenstretiger moved across the room, surely, silently, gripping Garcia's had firmly. There was a brief moment of eye contact, then Muenstretiger broke the moment and walked over to the sideboard. "Wine?" He broke open a bottle and began pouring before Garcia could reply. He looked up, his eyes twinkling. "I understand you appreciate wine."

"Yes, sir, although I can't afford thousand-dollar bottles."

"Well, this is just a mediocre Sirency." He brought the wine over and gestured to the chairs. "I hate to rush you, but I really don't have much time and this is going to take a while. I think you'll be quite interested."

"Frankly, I can't see why you'd be interested in showing me anything."

Muenstretiger smiled. "Well, to tell the truth, it was my daughter's idea. But, for once, I think she's right." He pressed some buttons on his chair, the room darkened, and a holo appeared in the middle of the room, in front of them. It showed a large white laboratory rat. "How old would you say this animal was, Garcia?"

"I'm afraid I don't know very much about animals. Ten years?"

Muenstretiger raised an eyebrow. "Not bad. Actually, it's twelve years old, which is nearly four times the age at which a laboratory rat would normally die of old age. Not that many of them *do* die of old age."

"You've discovered some kind of immortal rat? I don't really care, to tell you the truth."

"No, I don't expect you to have any interest in rats. But *I* do. I run the largest pharmaceutical concern in the world, and we use a lot of rats." Muenstretiger smiled. "Some of them even work for me. But this rat is, as you have suggested, probably immortal."

"Probably?"

"Who knows when it will die? But it's not a special strain of rat, Garcia. We have obtained similar results with monkeys and pigs."

"You have monkeys and pigs working for you too?"

Muenstretiger smiled again. "You know where I'm leading, Garcia?"

"Immortality. For man."

"Not for any man, Garcia. For you."

Garcia squirmed in his chair. "I'm afraid not. I don't want to become one of your lab animals."

Muenstretiger held up a hand. "I'm not suggesting that. We've already performed the operation on several dozen human beings. It's not experimental."

"But you can't be certain it works. Not after only ten years."

"Less than that. The first operation on a human being took place a little over a year ago. Let me tell you what's involved. Then you'll have a better understanding with which to make your decision."

"How much do you charge people for this experiment?"

Muenstretiger smiled. "For those who can afford it, quite a lot. But for you, Garcia, nothing. After all, you're an artistic treasure and I feel you should receive the operation before it's too late."

An artistic treasure? Was he already carved in granite? "What do you mean, too late."

Muenstretiger sighed. "Come on." He stood up. "I'll show you through our laboratory and then you'll understand."

They went to a large building at the back of the estate, where they were greeted by an intense tiny man with a scraggly fringe of a beard. "This is Dr. Gregg. He'll explain the procedure to you. I'll see you later in my study."

"Ah, Garcia! A pleasure, a pleasure." Dr. Gregg pumped Garcia's hand enthusiastically. "How much has Muenstretiger explained to you?"

"Not very much, I'm afraid."

"Good. Well, I won't go into the details of how we discovered the process. Let me merely say that it was a matter of serendipity and some brilliant leaps of logic, in which I am proud to say I had a small part, and Muenstretiger gave us his full and complete support."

"I'm sure."

"This way, please." Dr. Gregg led him to a small operating room, oblivious to Garcia's discomfort. "The first thing we do is excise a small portion of your thymus gland."

"That sounds painful."

"Oh, no. We can do it without even leaving a scar." The doctor showed Garcia a small tube about a quarter of a meter in length made of clear plastic. "We merely insert this into your body and it slides quite easily through the tissues. Then we can insert microsamplers inside it. We don't need much tissue. Come on, I'll show you."

Dr. Gregg next took Garcia to a large laboratory where technicians worked at incomprehensible tasks. "This is where we divide and culture our tissues. Over here, for example, we have those of Shaara and Mont'Illiano." The masses of tissue seemed obscene and disgusting to Garcia.

"They are going to be, uh, immortal?" he asked.

"Oh, certainly. All the major families are having their children cultured. Now, after we've cultured about twenty different samples, we send them to the Erestus facility for irradiation."

"Wouldn't that kill them or something?"

"Oh, yes, we lose most of our samples that way, nearly fifty percent. And most of the others either become cancerous or mutate in unacceptable ways. But there seems to be a tendency for the immortality mutation to occur spontaneously often enough that two or three samples are usually viable for our purposes."

"And if they don't?"

Dr. Gregg shrugged. "Then we have to take another sample and try again."

"What happens after you have good samples?"

"We culture a new gland from the samples and implant it in the original donor."

"That's all there is to it?"

"Oh, there are a lot of minor details, of course." Dr. Gregg patted Garcia's stomach. "Diet, for one thing. A restricted caloric intake has always been conducive to an extended life. But that's the broad outline."

Garcia felt he was missing something important but there was no way he could tell what it was. One of those "minor details" might, in fact, be very important.

$\wp\langle\rangle\wp$

Munstretiger was waiting for him in the study when Dr. Gregg returned him to the main house. "Well, how do you feel about it?"

Garcia shook his head. "I feel like my head's spinning and yet I feel I don't have all the details I need."

"Of course."

"For one thing, I still don't understand why you're offering this to *me*."

"I told you..."

"I know! But why not Bwire? He's much older, and he can't live much longer."

"I know. And that's the very reason why we can't help him. His body wouldn't be able to take the shock of the operations — rather than making him immortal, it would probably kill him. I'm sorry, Garcia." The industrialist was quiet for a moment then continued, almost apologetically. "You see, Shaara's mother thought a great of him. It was she who introduced me to his music. Bwire's music and Lupa are linked in my mind, and I wish it were possible to help him. But there's nothing we can do for him now." Muenstretiger looked at Garcia with a strange expression on his face. "So when Shaara asked me to offer it to you, his best-known pupil, it was impossible for me to say no. I hope you don't mind being my second choice."

Garcia's answer was a choked "No."

"She'll be having her own operation in about a month, as soon as her immortality gland is grown. I hope you'll agree to join us. You can help as she learns to control my organization." Muenstretiger smiled at the look on Garcia's face. "You didn't think she had that much steel in her, did you? Well, I had hoped for a son, but Shaara has proven to be the equal of any male in the business."

"No, it wasn't that." How could Garcia convey his feelings about the implicit assumption that he and Shaara would be partners? The thought had been in his own mind, but he didn't like the feeling of being herded toward it, without any say of his own in the matter. "But... what about you? Why should you hand control over to Shaara?"

"I won't live forever, Garcia."

"But haven't you..."

Muenstretiger shook his head. "The thymus gland atrophies after adolescence. That's the real reason why we can't help Bwire. We haven't been able to culture an immortality gland for anyone over thirty and we haven't always been able to cultivate one for anyone over twenty-four."

"But I'm twenty-eight."

"That's why you should start immediately. It may already be too late for you."

Chapter 11

Garcia sat in his darkened apartment, looking at the screen in one wall, where the score Tattnall's *Savannah River Suite* was projected. It would be a show piece for his opening concert in the city; it was always a favorite here. But he wondered if it would be worth continuing with it for the rest of his tour. The rushing music of its beginnings, like the headwaters of the river in the southeastern mountains, became majestic in a way that might be boring to other audiences. He would have to talk to Renard about it. Renard had a much better feel for such things; he was more in tune with audience tastes. The agent would be surprised if Garcia asked him about it; usually, Garcia would tell him what music he planned to perform and then Renard would tell him which pieces would not be received well at certain concert sites. Then usually Garcia went ahead and performed them anyway and, more often than not, Renard would be proven right. Garcia didn't know how the agent did it, but he had a talent for predicting audiences. They would make a much better team if Garcia listened to him often; he resolved to do so in the future, wondering even as he made the resolution if he would be able to keep it.

Once, however, Garcia had the audience in his hands, he was usually able to flow with the energy, shaping it as he did so to his own direction and desires. It would be so much easier if he listened to Renard and played music that would get the audience and him in tune with each other much sooner.

He keyed in the music for Millen's *Weeping Willow* and practiced it for over an hour, working over the difficult passages and key changes until he had them down pat. It wasn't difficult; he hadn't played the music in over six months, but it all came back very rapidly. He decided to play a medley of *grilly* songs, beginning with the self-reflective humor of "Money Day" and ending with the mournful yet hopeful "Day Pages."

Carter's *Peanut Farm* would also be interesting, despite its local interest. It was a new addition to his repertoire. He went through it once, just to keep in practice. He had been practicing it regularly since his last concert series. Carter, although not an autar player himself, had written a moderately difficult run of thirty-second notes at the same time that the computer had to be reprogrammed three times in the space of twelve bars, including a major key change and a major change in rhythm. It had taken Garcia five months to master it to the point where he was willing to use the piece in a performance, and he prided himself on the knowledge that he was probably the only practicing autar player who was capable of performing it. Even at his peak, it might have been beyond Bwire's capabilities. Bwire himself claimed that he could never have done it, but Garcia had his doubts. The old man often played down his own ability.

They would round out the compositions Garcia had already told Renard he would be performing. With the other compositions, Garcia could juggle the piece to fit the audience and his mood, and no two performances would contain the same selections unless he wanted it that way.

"Garcia, I have a call from a Mr. Jack Orion. Will you take it?"

Jack Orion? What could he want? Despite his dislike for the commentator, Garcia couldn't very well refuse the call. He'd been lucky so far. Orion had not tried to tear him down. If he offended him now...

"Garcia! I'm glad I caught you in." Jack Orion's vulpine features grinned eagerly at Garcia.

"Can I help you with something, Orion?" Garcia asked cautiously.

"I don't know. I hope so." Garcia wondered whether the confusion was genuine or feigned, a trap. "There's something going on and I don't know what it is. I don't like that. I thought maybe you could help me."

"I doubt it. I don't keep in contact with much except the world of music, and I don't think that would make very good news for you."

"But you were at the party the other night and... well, there was something in the air, a kind of expectancy, like they were celebrating something special."

"I didn't sense it."

Orion shook his head. "No, I guess you wouldn't. It was your first time there. But, listen, you know how we got separated after the party?"

"Yes."

"Well, you may not realize it, but it was deliberate." Garcia tried to look quizzical. "I have my sources, and I know that Mont'Illiano did it deliberately. He's trying to hide something from me."

Garcia shook his head. "He didn't tell me anything that he might want to hide from you."

Orion stared at Garcia, the air of confusion gone. "Tell me what happened after you left me."

Garcia told Orion what had happened, carefully excising what Mont'Illiano had told him about Jack Orion. It seemed that Orion was a bit freer than Mont'Illiano thought.

"That's all?"

"I think I've told you everything important."

Orion worried at his lower lip with his forefinger and thumb. "If you remember anything else, let me know." Garcia nodded. "Or if you hear anything that might help me. Remember, the *barraque* is counting on you, Garcia. You're one of us."

"I'm just a musician, Orion."

Jack Orion smiled. "You're more than you think, Garcia. Be sure to let me know if you remember anything important." He broke the connection and left Garcia alone with his thoughts.

He sat in the still-darkened room for a long moment, feeling like a pawn in some game whose rules he didn't understand. Both sides claimed him as one of theirs, yet he felt he didn't belong to either of them.

"Supervisor?"

"Yes?"

"What do you think about immortality?"

After a brief pause, the supervisor asked, "Could you be more specific? What do you wish to know about immortality?"

"Do you think it's a good idea?"

"I find no value judgment attached to it. Do you speak of physical immortality or that of fame?"

"Physical immortality."

"It is a hypothetical subject. In either case, the immortality is in truth limited."

"Limited?"

"Entropy assures us that fame eventually will end and the famous will be forgotten, since everything physical will end and all energy will become static."

"But what about longevity?"

"The oldest known human being lived to an age of one hundred and ninety-five years. He was Dewey Rose, who died in 2452. There are some alive today who may well pass that age in the near future, but the average life span is less than one hundred years, ninety-eight point seven to be precise. Extreme measures along with excellent heredity are required for longevity in excess of one hundred and twenty-five years."

"But suppose it were possible for people to live indefinitely. Would that be a wise idea?"

After a pause longer than that programmed into the supervisor, it said, "Several centuries ago Professor Michael Conrad of the University of Michigan in one of his early biological growth models accidentally included the assumption of immortality. The model stabilized at a point where no reproduction was occurring, no exploration was being made by the individual organisms into other spaces, even though those spaces were highly suitable for them. They were devoting all their resources to maintaining themselves." There was another pause. "I would not consider that to be beneficial."

Chapter 12

Garcia didn't see Jorme again until several days later, when they met at the auditorium where their first concert together was to be performed that night. The youngster was obviously on edge over the performance but Garcia had other things on his mind—he was busy tuning the auditorium.

"Is this really necessary?" Jorme asked as they entered the auditorium after conferring with the producer and Renard, as well as a small, red-bearded technician with whom Garcia seemed to be on close terms. "An analyzer would do a much better job, wouldn't it? How could you improve on its judgment?"

"Don't rely on machines too much." Another technician was onstage, where Jorme and Garcia would be later. Garcia activated his implanted receiver and said, "Give me a 440." The technician plucked a string on the autar. "The analyzer is a brute force device," he explained to Jorme, "relying primarily on pure tones. It sets up the major tuning of an auditorium but it's deaf to nuances."

They walked slowly around the auditorium, checking the volume of the autar's various notes. Occasionally Garcia asked for a change in the volume, but he waited until he had walked through the entire auditorium before he began to make the more delicate tuning. Then he would spend long moments at one spot, talking to the red-bearded technician, who now was at his spot with the computer at the back of the auditorium, delicately modifying the auditorium's acoustics to Garcia's specifications, while the technician onstage played different notes on the autar.

"This isn't going to do *me* any good," Jorme complained. "It's tuned to *your* instrument, not mine."

Garcia grinned. "You'll get your chance someday, don't worry." He stopped at the top of the center aisle. "Give me a little boost on the 550." The volume of the pitch began to rise. "Hold it. There. No, back it down a little. That's good. Okay, let's hear the 440 again."

Finally Garcia was satisfied and they walked back out to the lobby, where Renard and the producer were discussing business details.

"Are you finished?" Renard asked. "Then go home and get some rest. You've got five hours to the performance."

"Don't fool around with my auditorium while I'm gone."

"What do you think I am, crazy?"

As they walked to the waiting cab the producer had provided, Jorme asked, "Do you mind if I spend the rest of the time with you?"

"You'll probably drive me crazy with your nervousness."

"I'll try not to."

"Sure." If Jorme was left to himself, he would probably be a nervous wreck by concert time. Garcia would have preferred to be alone but the necessity of calming Jorme was one more cross he had to bear, now that he was a teacher.

But Jorme's mind was on other things. The cab had barely begun its journey through the streets when the young autarist blurted out, "What do you think of Pentland LaCroix?"

Ah-ha! Garcia grinned. "So that's why I saw so little of you the other night." Jorme's face turned beet red. "Is she as good in bed as she is to look at?"

Jorme shook his head. "I couldn't talk about things like that."

"Always the gentleman, eh?" Jorme was silent. "So just what is it you want me to say?"

"I don't know. It's all so confusing."

Garcia sighed. It was incredible that Jorme should be so innocent and naïve. He wondered if Bwire had considered that when he had sent Jorme to him. If Jorme had been as Garcia had been when he was still a student at the conservatory, there would have been instant friction between them. They would have been competitors and rivals, not the teacher and his protégé they had so easily become.

He wondered if he should exchange intimacy for intimacy and tell Jorme about the immortality offer. As Pentland LaCroix had been disturbing Jorme, the immortality offer had been disturbing Garcia. It was a strong temptation, yet for some reason it disturbed him. He was twenty-eight years old, by no means an old man, but not exactly young either. His mortality was beginning to lie on him, not heavy yet, but perceptible. Death was a long way off, but for the first time he could see it, and the years between suddenly seemed few. The approaching end of Bwire's life only sharpened that awareness.

When they reached Garcia's apartment, Garcia poured out some wine and sipped it meditatively while Jorme drank it in large gulps. "Not too much now," Garcia cautioned as he poured a second glass for Jorme. "You don't want to be drunk for tonight's performance."

"I don't? I'm so nervous I don't think I could even hold an autar, much less play one. I might do better if I was so drunk I didn't care."

"Nonsense. You've been through this before."

"No." Jorme shook his head emphatically. "No, I haven't. I have never before performed on the same stage as Garcia. I'm afraid they'll boo me off the platform."

"Don't worry about it."

"Don't worry about it, don't worry about it. How can I *not* worry about it?" Jorme began to pace the room, his large ungainly hands moving incessantly.

"Think about something else."

"What?"

"I don't know... Wait a minute." Garcia went to his library, finally choosing a cassette that didn't match any of the others in the library, and inserted it into the flat television and turned it on.

"What is it?" Jorme asked.

The screen lit up and they were looking at an old man... not as old as Bwire but older than Garcia... playing a very early model autar. The playing was ragged and imprecise; even the most inept student at the conservatory could do better—but his playing possessed a power and a strength that surpassed that of Jorme or Garcia.

"Who is it?" Jorme asked in a low intense whisper, as if the autarist on the tape could hear him and be interrupted.

"Racliffe."

"How...?"

"It was one of Stella Blue's possessions. She left it to me."

A man grown old and haggard before his time played on an ancient autar. His technique was clumsy and simplistic, but there was a raw power that could not be denied. When he was finished, the audience that had been watching him applauded for a long time. He stood before them, his gray-streaked head bowed. The camera moved closer, and Garcia and Jorme could see the lines, the crow's feet, the despair.

The screen grew dark. "That was his last concert." Garcia's voice was soft and subdued. "The film was taken by one of the timedippers."

"Stella Blue?" Jorme's voice was almost a whisper.

Garcia understood. There was something in Radcliffe's performance that was monumental and timeless, immortal, despite its simplicity. Or perhaps because of it.

"No. She had been cashiered out by then, because of her involvement with him. One of her friends took the film for her."

Jorme shook his head. "God. I wish I could play like that."

Garcia smiled. "So do I, Jorme. So do I."

Chapter 13

Jorme's nervousness disappeared when they reached the auditorium, but it was not replaced with an easy acceptance of the situation—instead he became a stiff, wooden zombie. Garcia's own nervousness before a performance, which he refused to admit even existed, was heightened by his concern for Jorme: if Garcia was nervous, Jorme was absolutely frightened. Even Pentland LaCroix was unable to do anything and they both watched helplessly from the stage wings as the youngster finally walked out in front of the audience.

By the time he sat down on the stage with his instrument, however, all traces of nervousness had sloughed off him and Jorme seemed as calm and composed as if he were playing in his own room. He was wearing garments of an identical cut to those of Garcia, although his were of a deep blue while Garcia's were a dark wine in color.

Jorme touched the autar and began his performance with Dark's *Elysian Visions*. For the next forty minutes, Garcia empathized with each semiquaver out of pitch, with each slightly-ragged tempo. But, if the performance lacked the precision that Garcia could have desired, it had enough power and strength to steamroller over most objections. Jorme need make apologies to no one.

At last the performance was over, Jorme took his bows and walked calmly offstage, his garments dripping with sweat, to receive Garcia's embrace. "Marvelous, Jorme, simply marvelous. See? You didn't have anything to worry about."

"None of us back here were worried," Renard said sarcastically.

"God! I thought it would never end. Did you hear that flub in the third movement of the Danbury Sonata?"

"You covered well. Only a handful of people would have noticed it. Maybe only you and me."

Jorme looked at Garcia quizzically. "Isn't that enough?" He looked around. "Is there something to drink back here? I'm dying of thirst." A stagehand thrust a container of liquid in his hand. It contained minerals and salts to replenish those that Jorme had lost. He took a long drink form it then turned to Garcia, grinning. "You're next."

᪥ < > ᪥

During the intermission Garcia called Bwire. "Did you catch Jorme's performance?"

"Excellent. He's definitely improved his technique under you, Garcia. That little thing he did in the Danbury Sonata reminded me of one of *your* early concerts." Garcia felt himself blushing. "You're an excellent teacher."

"More than that. His attitude is changing." Garcia told him about the brief interchange backstage when Jorme's performance was over. Bwire smiled. "Would you like to congratulate him?"

"Certainly."

While Jorme talked to the old master, Garcia wondered whether or not he should tell Bwire about the immortality offer. Now wasn't the time, of course; he would have to wait until he was alone with Bwire. But wouldn't it be cruel to tell Bwire that he'd been granted immortality when Bwire himself was so close to death?

Garcia walked back to the terminal when Jorme beckoned to him.

"I have been thinking, Garcia." Bwire paused and looked at him shrewdly. "My transcription of the Harrigan sonata seems to be lacking. I've made a few notes. I'll send them over to you. I'd like you to patch it up for me."

"The sonata is brilliant, Bwire!" Garcia objected.

"Nonetheless, I have a few ideas for making it more brilliant. I'd like you to look at them."

Garcia agreed to do so, then broke the connection.

"Maybe you ought to do some transcriptions of your own," Jorme suggested.

"I'm not a composer," Garcia growled. "Performing's enough work as it is."

"I thought you enjoyed performing."

Garcia punched Jorme playfully on the shoulder. "Do you have to pick up on every contradiction I make?"

"Five minutes," Renard said.

Garcia uncased his autar and powered it up, checked the tuning, and began running scales and exercises, flexing his fingers. The producer looked at him when he paused, and Garcia nodded.

"Two minutes," the producer said. The houselights dimmed slowly and brightened back up several times, and the audience began to filter back into the house.

"Who's running the show tonight?" Garcia asked.

"Steinbrunner," the producer replied.

Garcia smiled. "He's a good man."

"The best."

In a booth at the back of the auditorium, the red-bearded technician, Steinbrunner, was running the computer that controlled the lights, the sets, the sound, and everything else associated with the technical end of the theatre. The holocameras that were mounted discreetly in the ceiling and in small boxes in the footlights would be controlled by the technician, although the final transmissions would be determined by the producer. Like Garcia, Steinbrunner was a perfectionist, disgruntled whenever he made the slightest mistake, even though no one but he might know the difference.

The producer signaled to Garcia and he walked out onto the stage. The spotlight caught him a millisecond after he emerged from the wings and followed him faithfully to the comfortable chair at center stage.

Despite what he told Jorme and everyone else, Garcia was always nervous before a performance, although he usually was unaware of it himself. There was a warmth in his chest, a fear, and he became unusually animated so that Renard was always trying to calm him down. The first few moments of the performance were always the most fretful.

While the applause was dying, Garcia checked his tuning once more then began a slow moody piece which gradually accelerated until there was an eight-bar arpeggio central section. Meanwhile the computer backed him with a syncopated rhythm and chords in associated minors. As he moved into the arpeggio section, he reset the computer to a simple rhythm then back again as the music died.

Meanwhile the white spotlight which had engulfed him slowly faded while a soft blue haze from the stage lights rose until he was surrounded in a blue that turned metallic in the arpeggio section. The crossfade was done flawlessly and imperceptibly and, when the piece was finished, Garcia was bathed in an intense blue-white.

He followed with one of Bwire's transcriptions of a minor Twentieth-century composer, a brief composition of Arca's, and then changed the mood with a medley of *grilly* tunes. The computer picked up a harsh edge, stumbling as it tried to follow Garcia's rapid tempo changes. The stumbles were not accidental, but it took an accomplished autarist to keep the computer that confused, without losing the rhythm entirely. To prove that it was not accidental, Garcia ran through the changes three times, producing the exact same stumble each time.

Steinbrunner followed Garcia's performance with appropriate lighting, the *grilly* medley accompanied by constantly changing swirls of color, predominantly yellows and reds.

Even before he was finished, the *grilly* medley brought the audience to its feet, shouting and yelling. A few of the younger people tried to dance to the music.

The final piece was Bwire's *Wine Variations*, a long sonata whose mood changed from the bubbliness of champagne to the deep moodiness of a rich burgundy. Steinbrunner's lighting followed the mood, with claret shades predominant. Garcia had pushed himself quite far during the *Wine Variations*, so he settled for a very simple and straightforward encore.

He could still hear their applause when he finally left the stage unwillingly, not wanting to come back to the mundane world, barely feeling Renard's hand on his arm, hearing the congratulations and words, but unable to make any sense of them. He was guided to the backstage couch and a glass placed in his hand and practically guided to his mouth.

"Brilliant, Garcia. I swear, every time I think you can go no further, and yet you keep surpassing yourself." It was Mars Ruby. How much longer could he surpass himself? How long would it be before he merely rested on his reputation?

"Steinbrunner," he said in a voice that was surprisingly thick. "Where is he?"

The producer smiled. "You won't see him tonight, Garcia. You know that."

Garcia nodded. The little, red-bearded technician rarely came backstage after a performance. He was rarely seen even during rehearsals. He stayed in his tiny room at the back of the auditorium, watching his dials and controls, guiding his computer through its intricate paces. When the theatre was empty, he would come out to move the lights and other stage pieces where he wanted them, where the theatre machinery could locate them and aim them precisely.

Was he up there even now, waiting for everyone to leave, so he could be alone with his theatre mistress? Or had he already slipped out through his private entrance, mingling with the departing audience, unseen and unnoticed? And yet, without his artistry and craft, the performance would have had much less impact.

The whole theatre and performing world sometimes seemed to be a world of freaks and cripples: Garcia himself, so isolated in his apartment, isolated from reality throughout his whole life, so when he had met Stella Blue his defenses were barely formed; Jorme, so shy and insecure, and yet, in a way, much more worldly than Garcia had been at his age, or perhaps was even now, a workingman's son without the knowledge of the social graces so necessary in the circles where Garcia moved, and yet so cognizant of the larger world outside those circles; Mars Ruby, courtesan of the arts, a moderately-talented librettist herself, who nonetheless was best known for her bedroom liaisons with famous artists; Renard, a man who trusted no one and yet wanted to trust someone desperately but was afraid to do so, sour and sarcastic, building walls between himself and those who could become close to him; Justin Mead and his wife, both musicians with no common ground on which they could meet, performing different types of music, and trying to destroy each other, yet unwilling to separate; and poor Philip Steinbrunner, an enigma in the shell of his control room, a solitary figure whose only mistress and lover was the theatre itself.

Garcia's reverie was broken by a call from Bwire. "Excellent," the old master said. "You improve every time, Garcia. It was a new composition you played tonight; it wasn't what I thought I had written."

"I played every note in your score," Garcia protested.

Bwire smiled. "You misinterpret me. You played what I wrote and more. You reached beyond me and I appreciate it."

Garcia shook his head. "I didn't add anything to it. It was everything you wrote; it was there in the score."

"Perhaps you should compose something yourself, Garcia. Then you would know what I mean, when you heard someone else play it."

Garcia regained his composure and smiled at the old man. "I'm not a composer, Bwire."

"Why not? You have all the knowledge, and more than most composers. No matter. I have to get my beauty sleep. Convey my congratulations once more to Jorme. He has a good teacher and I'm proud of both of you."

"Thank you, Bwire."

Garcia stood there for a moment, thinking that he and Jorme were more children and family to Bwire than his own flesh-and-blood daughter, who knew nothing about music and cared less.

"What are we standing around for?" Renard asked. "It's party time."

Chapter 14

Garcia would have preferred to stay where he was, performing in his own familiar auditorium instead of traveling from city to city for several weeks. Although he wasn't paranoid about the transplats, they still made him nervous after all these years. He had never been able to verify any of the stories about people coming out of the transplat all scrambled: they were apocryphal, the stuff of nightmares and childhood terrors. Nonetheless, he distrusted the machines.

Some people claimed they felt a moment of disorienting darkness in the transmission interval, ghosts passing at light speed through optic fibers, crosstalking to each other, but Garcia had never felt a thing. He just walked into the booth and sat there a few moments, watching the warning light turn red, warning him not to leave the booth, then quickly turn green again. When he left the booth, there would be a different attendant and the city outside the doors of the transplat terminal would be different. It would be nice if he left it slim and slender and suave but that was even less likely than coming out scrambled. Things were best as they were.

When he had been Jorme's age, he had enjoyed the travel, exploring each city eagerly, if a bit superficially, but now they had all become the same, and the joy and taste of each was gone. Each had its own version of the *barraque*, its rich section, its artistic bohemian quarter, its business section (where the auditoriums were usually located), and its sections where the middle-incomers and the rising well-to-do lived. The details changed from city to city but, after a while, they all merged into one featureless blur. Better to get to know one city well than to sample a little of each, but never get to know any of them deeply.

Even the auditoriums, once the central focus of his existence, were beginning to merge, until he was astonished that the details of Casablanca were not found in Madrid, when the remaining oriental features of Hong Kong and Tokyo surprised him.

Jorme, on the other hand, was eager to explore Paris, the site of their next concert. Was it possible that he had never left the confines of his own city? Jorme blushed and admitted he had only been out of the city twice, and then only for a short time.

"Where did you go?" Garcia asked.

"The Rocky Mountain park. Have you ever been there?"

Garcia shook his head. "No. To tell the truth, I've never been out of the city complexes."

Jorme regarded him oddly. "Haven't you ever had any desire to visit the parks?"

"No. Why should I?"

"Just to experience them. They're so different from the cities. You can't imagine what they're like."

"Breathing raw air and far from the nearest convenience? No thanks."

"You don't know how exhilarating raw air can be. And the conveniences aren't *that* far away. They're no further away than they are in the *barraques*."

"I've been through that once, Jorme. Not again."

Nonetheless he went with Jorme through the ancient city, which was now more museum than city, to the fabled Antoine's, where traditional ancient musicians played traditional ancient music on traditional ancient instruments, raw and full of impure tones, the harmonics from the horns grating on the ear. Even Jorme complained that the music was painful to listen to.

"Once all music was that way," Garcia said. "Even the original autars didn't play as precisely as we're used to. There were lots of spurious harmonics."

"How could they stand it?"

"They thought it was beautiful."

Jorme shook his head sadly.

After dinner they strolled through Montmartre and the artists' quarter, apparently unchanged for a thousand years, although they both knew that most of the buildings had been recreated from old photographs and prints: they stopped for coffee at the Louvre, where artists hawked prints of the Eiffel Tower, the Statue of Liberty, and Notre Dame; they walked through the Tuileries, the Bastille, and Versailles, all recreated from their most flowering periods; they watched fandango dancers and apache dancers on the streets of the Left Bank.

Shaara was waiting for Garcia in his room when they returned to their hotel.

"What are you doing here?" he asked.

"Renard let me in." She smiled coquettishly.

He smiled back, pleased and strangely touched. "I wish I'd known you were coming. I hope you didn't wait long."

"Oh, that's all right. I enjoyed it."

She moved toward him and, for a long moment, there were no more words between them.

"You know, you act toward Jorme like a father, and you're not even thirty years old yet."

"Do I?" The thought bothered Garcia, and yet it also had a kind of charm to it.

"Yes. You're not like that with other musicians, are you?"

"Hardly. I've always been kind of separate, even at the conservatory. Other kinds of musicians, like Justin Mead, didn't bother me. But I didn't like being near other autarists."

"Competition?"

"Maybe. I'm not sure"

"They must have thought were some kind of a snot."

Garcia grimaced. "Yeah. I guess they did."

"But you were better than any of them, weren't you?"

"Not when I started I wasn't. I mean, I was younger than anyone else but I still had a lot to learn. I guess I *was* kind of a snot, though. I thought it was going to be easy."

"Was it?"

"Most of it was." Perhaps that was the trouble. Perhaps it had all come *too* easy. He had come to the end of the road and there were no challenges left, no new roads to conquer.

They lay there together for a long moment, slowly caressing each other.

Pentland LaCroix joined them in Rome, and the two couples toured the ancient city together. Although it was far older than Paris, it was still alive and full of people, not a museum, an epitaph to the past, as Paris had become. The old buildings of the Roman Empire, the Coliseum, the viaducts, all the buildings that had stood for two thousand years, were worn and eroded by the acid rains from the polluted air of the Twentieth century. All that remained of the Coliseum was a small bank of seats, now encased in a hermetic block of glassite, to be viewed but not touched. Nearby, a four-foot-diameter model showed the Coliseum had looked like in its prime.

"It's sad, in a way, you know?" Pentland said. "All the great buildings of the past are gone."

"We have their reconstructions," Garcia said.

"It's not the same." Pentland stared moodily at the model. "Think what it must have been like to stand in the center of the Coliseum with thousands of people around you, *thousands*, in the flesh, to cheer you while you performed."

"Or boo you, or throw vegetables or worse."

"Besides," Jorme said, "they didn't perform at the Coliseum. They were sacrificed or fed to the lions."

"And the Globe Theatre," Pentland continued, her eyes focused on some distant dream.

"The what?" Garcia asked.

"The Globe Theatre. Where Shakespeare performed."

"Is that in Rome?" Garcia asked.

"You guys!" Pentland's mouth was twisted into a wry smile. "You don't have any culture."

But it *was* sad to think of those buildings that had survived so long and yet had succumbed so rapidly to civilization. How many generations separated Garcia from Julius Caesar? Hundreds. If Julius Caesar were alive today, would he weep for the vanished Coliseum? Or would he just build another of the day's evanescent buildings? The auditorium where Garcia performed would someday be gone, just like the coliseum. It probably would not last nearly as long.

In Hong Kong, Garcia found himself alone with Pentland LaCroix for a few moments. They had spent so much time together, Jorme and Pentland, Garcia and Shaara, young lovers enjoying the cities, enjoying themselves, a double cocoon over them, friends and lovers. Frequently the two couples would separate and, as has happened since time immemorial, the two men and the two women would be alone together. But rarely had Garcia been alone with Pentland.

"Sometimes," she said, "you seem so aloof, as though you're somewhere else."

"I've never been very good at being with people." He found it hard to look her in the eye.

She smiled. "I didn't notice that at Muenstretiger's or after your concerts."

"Parties are different. I can perform there, but being alone with people, with friends, is a different thing and I don't always know how to act. Besides, you're all so much younger than me."

"Five years." Pentland cocked her head at him. "You're not an old man, Garcia."

"No, but you and Shaara and Jorme are all pretty much the same age and, well, sometimes I just find it hard to feel like I'm one with you all."

"Garcia!" She covered his hand with her slender one. "You *are* one of us and you certainly are not old." But already there were gray hairs. Was that a bad omen? Would his immortality gland not be viable? He dared say nothing to Shaara or to Muenstretiger.

"There you are! Stealing my girl, are you?" Jorme and Shaara came around the corner of the building, carrying presents for Garcia and Pentland.

༄⟨⟩༄

When they reached Nairobi for the last week of concerts, Shaara said, "This will be the last concert I'll be able to attend. It's time for my operation. I've got to leave tomorrow morning."

"When will…?" He stopped.

"I'll probably still be in the hospital when you return. You'll come to visit me, won't you?"

"Of course."

His performance that night was even more moving than usual, a blend of joy, sadness, expectation, and doubt. He added the Radcliffe sonata for the first time during the tour, his mind full of the young girl who had truly introduced him to the inventor of the autar. The technician at Nairobi was no Steinbrunner, but he was competent and Garcia was able to fill the hall with his emotions.

Chapter 15

The final concert of their tour was to be in their home city again. Garcia had paid little attention to the critics during the tour, although Jorme came to him with each little carp and cavil, each praise and adulation. Most of the praise was for Garcia, although every two-bit critic had to find some fault, however minor, with his performance. Jorme had not fared as well but most of the critics were kind, content to damn him with such faint praise as, "In time, Jorme will be in the same class as his teacher."

Jorme took the criticism hard, as Garcia had been afraid he would, but he managed to perform credibly nonetheless, and Garcia was certain that in time he would be as inured to the critics as Garcia had become. There was only one critic to whom Garcia ever listened, the academician Elnor, who had been disappointed by the change in Garcia's style after the death of Stella Blue. Elnor's obsession, as Garcia's had once been, was technique and precision. He could not deny Garcia's still crisp technique but he did not understand the passion. Garcia was afraid that he would tear poor Jorme to bits, for Jorme's forte was power and passion, although his technique improved with each performance.

Elnor apparently had not attended the first concert, for there had been no review from him. Perhaps he was saving himself for the final concert.

Garcia had heard nothing from Shaara during the last two concerts and, despite her assurances, he was worried. He fidgeted all the time, unwilling to make a panic call while Jorme and Renard were around. But, as soon as he was alone, he placed a call to Muenstretiger's residence. After passing thorough three levels of servants and secretaries, he finally found himself face to face with the industrialist

"Ah, yes. Have you decided to accept our offer, Garcia?"

"Certainly. I'll undergo the first operation as soon as my final concert is over. But that's not why I called you."

"You'd like to talk to my daughter. I'll have her contact you as soon as possible."

Garcia's panic and worry rose even further; were there some complications with her operation? "When will that be?"

"Oh, it shouldn't be long. I'll have one of my men contact her and she should call you back within the hour. Probably less. Hang on." Garcia watched while Muenstretiger talked to one of his subordinates on another line. He turned back to Garcia, smiling. "All right. Let me put you in contact with DeLuc. He'll make an appointment for the first operation."

A few seconds later, one of Muenstretiger's subordinates appeared and Garcia made an appointment for the day after his final concert. "We'll send a limousine for you," the subordinate said, and broke the contact.

Garcia stared unseeing at the now-empty room. Was that all there was to it? Was it that simple to become immortal? No, that was just the start. But with a few simple words he had committed himself to the whole process. How easy it was to change the whole course of your life, not even knowing if it was the right thing to do.

Why... *why* did he feel so uneasy about accepting Muenstretiger's offer? He should have jumped at it. Instead he kept coming up with excuses for delaying the process and avoiding it. Perhaps in a couple of years. But by then it might already be too late; his thymus gland would be gone, absorbed by his body and his chance at immortality forever departed.

There was a soft chime and the supervisor announced Shaara's call.

"Garcia! You're back." There was no projected image in the middle of the room.

"Shaara. Where are you? Let me see you."

"No. Not yet. Not in bed." Did he detect an edge of panic, of fear, in her voice? "Not in a hospital bed." She laughed briefly and it sounded hollow and brittle to Garcia.

"Oh, come now." He found his attempt at joviality to be an effort. "You can't look that bad. Where are you?"

"Infants Grove. But you can't come to see me, Garcia."

"Why not? The operation hasn't changed your appearance, has it?"

"No, but... it's very closely guarded. You understand, don't you?"

"No, I don't!" It was the closest they'd come yet to having an argument. "Look, Shaara, I love you."

"You love a lot of women."

"Not the way I love you. Why can't I see you now?"

"Because, darling, I've just had an operation and the danger of sickness and contagion is..."

"Damn it, girl, that kind of thing was conquered long ago!"

"But we immortals don't take unnecessary chances. There's no sense in taking chances, however slight, with the loss of eternity at stake."

"Okay," Garcia grumbled.

"I've got to stop now, dear. Time for my beauty sleep. I'll watch your last concert on HV."

Garcia stared at the empty room, seeming emptier without even her voice. Was he that far gone? What was she? A rich man's daughter, with apparently mediocre talents. There were so many other more interesting and talented women who would be eager to share his life. His *life*! This wasn't for a few nights or even a few years, but a lifetime. And his life would stretch out into an unending future.

Of course that was ridiculous. It wasn't immortality they were talking about. Sooner or later, all these so-called "immortals" would die. But how long, how long into the interminable future before that day would come? So it was natural, perhaps, that they would take extraordinary measures against disease and accidental death. But it bothered him.

The supervisor chimed again, announcing a call from Jack Orion. Garcia hesitated before allowing the supervisor to complete the connection, but he felt he really had no choice. If Orion even so much as suspected what Garcia knew...

"Have you found out anything, Garcia?"

"About what?" Garcia let his uneasiness surface in irritation. That should be a safe emotion.

"I don't know what but I'll find out, damn it. Listen, it has something to do with Muenstretiger. He's very important and you're very close to him now, aren't you?"

"I've seen him only briefly since the party. I spend most of my time Shaara, not with him."

Jack Orion was quiet for a long moment and Garcia wondered what calculations were going on behind those shrewd eyes. "Yes, you've been seeing a lot of her, haven't you?"

"Yes, I have. What of it? We like each other."

"Garcia, she's one of *them*. Her father is grooming her to take his place when he dies."

"He's already told me that."

Orion's eyes seemed to pierce Garcia. "And where does that leave you? When she takes over his position, what will you do?"

Garcia sighed. "I'll cross that bridge when I come to it. I'm not an industrialist, Orion, I'm a musician. What Shaara does or doesn't do is no concern of mine."

Orion raised an eyebrow theatrically. "No? I'd say otherwise. Nonetheless, I'm expecting you to let me know if you learn anything important."

"Listen, Orion, neither you nor Shaara nor Muenstretiger nor anyone else own me. I don't have to take veiled threats from you or anyone else."

To Garcia's surprise, the commentator backed off. "I didn't mean to threaten you, Garcia." His tone was oily and placating. "I'm just reminding you. I don't have any power, Garcia." Garcia thought otherwise but said nothing. "Well, if you have nothing to tell me, I'll leave you alone. But I hope you'll think over what I've said and please don't hold anything back. We're all counting on you."

Garcia started at the empty holostage, both hands, artificial and real, clenched into useless fists.

Chapter 16

Bwire appeared more withered and sere than he had just a few weeks earlier, as though he had aged years in that short time. If ever there was a reason for Garcia to accept the offer of immortality, it was sitting in front of him. And yet Garcia felt guilty that Bwire would never know immortality.

His skin was the color of old suede, mottled and a dull leathery tan. He did not rise from the chair, but motioned weakly toward the chair opposite. As before, the nurse outside the room, monitoring the old master, had warned Garcia not to get him excited, that they could spend only a few minutes together.

"How are you feeling?" Garcia asked awkwardly.

"As well as could be expected. I'll live to see your concert tomorrow. I expect to enjoy it." The words were delivered almost as an ultimatum: I'd *better* enjoy it, the old man seemed to say, if you know what's good for you.

"Your nurse said I couldn't stay with you very long."

"I know, I know." Bwire waved a hand peevishly. "They say not to get excited then they do all they can to cause to get me exasperated and frustrated." Garcia waited, not knowing what to say. "Over there, over there." Bwire pointed to the cabinet on the far side of the room. "There are some papers. Bring them here."

Garcia walked over to the cabinet, finding a sheaf of music paper with notes scrawled over them. "These?"

"Yes. Bring them here. This is my Sonata for Autar and Flute. For you and Justin. It needs work. I want you to finish it."

"But... I can't do that."

"Who else?"

"I don't know anything about composing."

"Nonsense. You know more about music than most composers." Bwire looked up at Garcia and the harsh brown eyes seemed to soften. "Please," he said in a voice so gentle it pierced Garcia like an arrow made of neutrinos.

"I... I..." Bwire smiled at Garcia's uncharacteristic lack of words. "Why don't you keep it for now," Garcia said finally, "and I'll finish it for you when... if..."

"When I die," Bwire said calmly. "Face it, my friend. I have. Long ago."

"How can you...?"

"How can I not?" Bwire spread his hands in a gesture of resignation. "You saw how I was a couple of years ago. Frantic, frightened."

"No!"

"Yes. I was. Now. As you say, our time is limited. I accept your offer. Let us go over the score. Here. Can you read my scribbles?"

"Of course." Garcia had read Bwire's "scribbles" too many times in the past and, though the master's hand was shaky, it was still legible.

"Good. Now, I wanted to make a more intricate pattern for the computer here but I wasn't certain it could be programmed fast enough."

Garcia looked where the skeletal finger pointed. While the autarist was playing a series of arpeggios and the flute was soaring over the accompaniment in long glissandos, the computer's harmonics required a change in programming as the key altered through a series of sixth slides.

"Maybe if we let the computer do the sixths rather than the autar," Garcia suggested.

"I thought of that. But there would be a gap in the texture if the autarist was silent during the change."

"But if we preprogrammed the key change and activated the key change one string at a time, it would be possible to play single notes and two- or three-note chords on the open strings as the key changed, and stay in tune with the computer."

"Interesting. It can be done?"

"I think so."

"All right. Let's change the melody line for the performer then and let the computer handle the key change."

They worked together for nearly an hour, despite several interruptions from Bwire's nurse, who kept insisting that it was time for Garcia to leave. Each time Bwire waved her away, until at last she refused to take no for an answer.

Garcia looked at the closed door, wondering if he would ever see Bwire alive again. He wondered that each time he saw him, and one day it would happen. Would it be this time? He had wanted to talk to the nurse, find out how badly off Bwire really was, but she had stayed inside with him, shutting the door to any inquiry.

Goodbye. Sometimes it seemed that life was nothing but a constant series of goodbyes. And how many more, how infinitely many more goodbyes there would be if he were immortal. He had told no one, not Bwire, not Jorme, not Justin, not even Mars Ruby or Renard, about Muenstretiger's offer. How could he? He felt ashamed of being singled out and he didn't want to hear their false congratulations and see the envy and jealousy behind their masks. Bwire alone might understand and not be jealous... but Garcia did not have the heart to tell him. Bwire would never know; Garcia was determined of that.

Chapter 17

Garcia didn't see Jorme after they returned home until they met again for the final concert at the same auditorium where they had begun. It was a different Jorme that Garcia met, different from the Jorme who had been so nervous before his first concert with Garcia. It was the eager, puppyish Jorme with whom Garcia was so familiar who now showed up at the auditorium.

"You'll never guess what I did yesterday!" he announced as soon as he saw Garcia.

"What did you do yesterday?" Garcia knew, for Bwire had already told him.

"I went to the conservatory and, Garcia, it was incredible. They treated me like some kind of conquering hero."

"Well, you've put on quite a series of concerts. You've conquered the public and you've got a reputation now that can't help but grow."

"Well, it wasn't only me." The puppy exuberance turned into an awkward shyness. "Pentland was with me."

Garcia thought of berating the youngster for not showing up for the auditorium tuning that afternoon but decided to say nothing. He had accompanied Garcia to every other auditorium when it was tuned, and it must have become as boring to him as it had been to Garcia when Bwire had shown him how to tune an auditorium.

Jorme was eager for his last performance and he practically swaggered out onto the stage. The tour had definitely been good for his confidence. Even if he had received no rave reviews, at least most of them had been kind, and no one had chopped him to pieces. And several times he had been called back for second encores.

Tonight he would be performing Bishop's transcription of Ohana's Concerto for Guitar and Orchestra, the computer performing percussive effects with remarkable fidelity to the original. It would be the sum total of Jorme's final performance, except for the encores. Garcia watched from the wings, half nervous, half proud, grinning, sneaking glimpses at the monitor from time to time but keeping most of his attention on the live performance itself.

Pentland LaCroix was at his side, as nervous and proud as Garcia, and they exchanged only a few words, rapt in the youngster's performance. But Garcia was constantly aware of her presence. She wasn't the fluff-headed beautiful woman he originally had assumed her to be. There was a sharp mind behind those good looks and a gentle human being whose edges hadn't been honed to sharp points by the media and the pressures of the holovision world. If she could maintain her balance, she and Jorme might make a good pair.

Matchmaker! Now Garcia's smile was for himself. He was thinking about Jorme as though Jorme were his son, much in the same manner that Bwire treated Garcia.

Jorme finished a nearly flawless performance of the concerto and was called back for a second encore. Garcia hoped they would call him back for one more but the audience quieted down as soon as he finished the second one and began moving toward the lobby for the intermission.

Meanwhile the tension mounted in Garcia. He took the customary call from Bwire, talked with Jorme, congratulating him, checked the tuning of his autar and rechecked it, until finally the audience returned and he walked out on the stage again, calmness settling over him like a cloak.

Unlike Jorme, Garcia had chosen a series of brief pieces rather than one long one, terminating in Carter's *Peanut Farm*, which he had mastered still further on the tour, although there were a few passages he wasn't yet satisfied with. But it was strange how a piece that he performed so well and competently at home while practicing suddenly became alive and electric during a performance, a whole new piece with a life of its own. No, he wasn't like Jorme: he needed the crowds, the audience, the performance itself. This was when he felt most alive, emotions pulsing through him like electrical currents, his thoughts as swift and piercing as the calculations of any computer, his perceptions heightened until it seemed every note took on a crispness and brilliance that could never be equaled again. But there was the next one, as crisp and as brilliant.

This was what he lived for, this was his reason for existence. And yet... though the joy and excitement of performing were there and as sharp as ever (somehow subtly forgotten during the months when he didn't perform), there was a nagging doubt at the back of his mind. Was *this* really all there was to life? Wasn't there something else, something other than performing someone else's compositions, recreating, in effect someone else's emotions? While his mind was caught in the questions, his fingers performed like separate creatures until the concert was over, and it seemed it had barely begun.

It was all so anticlimactic, such a tremendous letdown, to be finished with performing once again. All the electricity, all the anticipation, and what was left? Nothing. A handful of recordings and a mind full of memories that would fade in time. And the cycle would be repeated again in another few months, and again, and yet again, for how long?

If he were immortal, he would have time for uncounted careers. He could become a physicist or an astronomer. Or could he? The autar had been his life since he was seven years old. Would it in time become boring? Would he reach the limits of the instrument or at least his own limits with it? Would everything become rote, a knotted snarl of reflexes? Just say "Bwire's last sonata" to him, like the computer, he'd be programmed to perform it, down to the last nuance, all emotion canned, all spontaneity drained.

Did he indeed have the talent, the intelligence, the capability to be anything other than a musician? He didn't care to be anything else now. But, in time, would he tire of the same old grind, over and over, repeated endlessly, until he'd lost count of the times, lost count, indeed, of the centuries? It seemed absurd and improbable and yet... would the edge go out of his life?

Don't look a gift horse in the teeth, he told himself, not really understanding why anyone would to look *any* animal in the teeth.

"Are you all right?" Pentland LaCroix's beautiful face hung over him.

"I'm fine. Just..."

"Drained?" He nodded. "I know how you feel. Sometimes I feel that way after a recording session."

He smiled in agreement but he wondered if it was the same. Could she ever really understand the solitude of the live performer? Her performance was distilled through many eyes and hands, those of the director and technicians, repeated again and again until they had what they wanted. Although Garcia's performance could be enhanced or marred by the hands of technicians such as Steinbrunner, nothing could save him from his own mistakes and imperfections. He had one shot each night and there were no retakes. Pentland LaCroix might be drained and exhausted at the end of a day's recording but the emotional load that Garcia and Jorme went through was something she would never know.

"I brought you some champagne." He took the glass gratefully and drained half of it, barely tasting it. "That was easily the best concert that you and Jorme have given. I hope they recorded it."

"They record all of them."

"But they couldn't capture the feeling of being right here and seeing the music made right before your eyes."

"No. No, they couldn't."

"Sometimes," she said wistfully, "I wish I was in live theatre. I envy you and Jorme so much, being able to put it all out on one line, one magnificent chance."

"You don't have any chances to correct mistakes." Garcia's voice was soft.

"No. You're naked out there. All on your own. It's all yours and no one can take that away from you."

"It can be frightening sometimes."

"Life always is. Or at least it should be. What's the sense in always doing the sensible thing, the safe thing? Sometimes I wish... sometimes I wish I were a musician rather than an actress."

Garcia took her hand. "Most musicians play in studios or, at best, in groups. There aren't many soloists who play live concerts anymore."

"Maybe... maybe I could do something live, like those poets at The Welcome Machine. Do you think they'd be interested?"

"I'm sure they'd love to have you perform."

Her smile was cynical. "They'd love to have me perform naked."

Garcia raised his eyebrows. "You can't blame them for that, can you?"

She laughed, a full-throated laugh that yet was as dainty as crystal, and pulled her hand free. "Well, I can see you've recovered from your depression. I think I'll go back to Jorme."

Garcia watched her sensuous departure, the graceful walk of an animal, tamed yet wild, civilized yet unspoiled.

Nearby, a young man sat in solitude, like Garcia, nursing his champagne. Garcia almost passed him by before he realized who it was.

"Philip! Come over and talk to me."

The young man, who had a ragged rust-red beard and watery gray eyes, moved over. "You looked busy." His soft friendly voice betrayed nothing of the shyness Garcia knew was there.

"You did a fine job tonight, Philip."

Philip shrugged. "It could've been better."

"You have nothing to be ashamed of."

Philip grinned suddenly. "Neither do you."

"What do you think of Jorme?"

"He's good, quite good. You'll have to watch out for him in a couple of years. He might take away your crown."

Garcia looked at his empty glass. "Sooner or later, someone's going to. It might as well be my own protégé. That would look a lot better."

There was a strange look in Philip's eyes as he regarded Garcia silently for a moment. "You're changing."

"Everyone changes."

"I'm glad. It's about time. First Stella Blue, and now Jorme."

And Shaara, Garcia thought, but he said nothing.

Philip closed the silence by asking about Bwire.

"He's dying, Philip. He's dying."

"I know. But is he dying well?"

Garcia looked at Philip, uncomprehending. "How can anyone die well?"

"Shakespeare said it once: 'Nothing became his life so well as the leaving of it.' Or something like that."

"But there's nothing I can do for him, Philip!"

"Sure there is. Just be there. Be his friend and his best student, as you've always been. That's all he asks; that's all he wants. Bwire's a good man, Garcia. He's very proud of you and he has every reason to be." Philip got up. "Well, I'd better be going. I've got to reset the lights for tomorrow night."

"You never stay at these things for very long."

"I'm not a very social person, I'm afraid. Parties get tedious and boring very rapidly."

"Philip." The technician looked at him, expectantly. "Do you know if Elnor reviewed tonight's performance?"

Philip nodded. "I'm sure he did. He was on the net."

"Okay. Thank you."

Garcia watched Steinbrunner leave, feeling a little sorry for the technician, yet not a great deal, for Steinbrunner obviously didn't feel very sorry for himself. In fact, Garcia reflected, he seemed to feel a little sorry for Garcia... who had more than Steinbrunner would ever have.

There was a blare of noise and Garcia was jolted out of his reflections again, this time by the holovision someone had turned on. The reception room had become a large life-size stage and they were trying to find the critical reviews of the concert.

Jorme and Pentland came over to Garcia, the youngster's dirty blond hair seeming unruly and unkempt next to the HV star's brilliant dark waves. But anyone with half an eye could see how much the two of them were in love. Garcia envied them: What he shared with Shaara was a cold passion compared to what the two of them had. Slowly, other people drifted over to be near Garcia and Jorme: Justin Mead and his wife, dowdy but talented; Mars Ruby and a young man whom Garcia had heard referred to as an up-and-coming plastic artist; Renard, escorting a plain lady who was probably some producer's secretary. Suddenly Garcia felt very lonely. He wished Shaara was out of the hospital and at his side.

The initial reviews all were very complimentary, picking on little details here and there, even on Steinbrunner's lighting at times. Some of them were embarrassingly gushy; even Jorme squirmed at the fulsome praise that was directed toward him.

Finally Elnor appeared on the stage. He was thin as a rail, almost to the point of emaciation, and he wore anachronistic spectacles that added to his scholarly air. Garcia had always wondered if they contained panes of ordinary glass.

"Ichabod Crane," someone muttered as Elnor peered out at his imaginary audience, as though he could actually see them. The critic was the master of the significant pause.

"Garcia and Jorme concluded their triumphant tour today with their second concert at the Radcliffe Memorial Auditorium. A full house of 402 was present in person, with a holovision audience rated at eight percent."

Elnor looked up from the sheaf of papers which he pretended to read and peered out at the viewers. "As I'm sure all of you know, Jorme is Garcia's first student and protégé. Before Garcia took him on as a pupil, Jorme had not given even a single solo concert, although he had been rated as one of the most promising students at the conservatory. Jorme has maintained his perfect record, since he has been sharing Garcia's concerts. It may be time that he went out on his own; it is not wise for Garcia to allow Jorme's mistakes to be forgotten in the wake of his own performances."

Elnor returned to his notes. "Jorme has improved immeasurably since his initial concert here at Radcliffe. The nervousness that was apparent the first night has disappeared from his performance. In its place, the emotion and fire have increased and are more in control. Nonetheless, the lack of precision and, in places, outright sloppiness..."

Garcia watched Jorme as Elnor savaged his performance. The jovial face took on a granitic stolidness, pain etched in the lines of his brow and around his eyes. Pentland, on the other hand, was a study of anger. She kept interrupting the holocast with exclamations of "That's not true!" and "He's crazy!" but Jorme stopped her simply by placing his hand on her shoulder.

Elnor then moved on to Garcia's own performance, which he praised quite openly while picking out every single failure of technique, not matter how minute, that Garcia himself had been aware of.

"It is to be hoped," Elnor concluded, "that Garcia's precision and technique will be mastered by his protégé, rather than Garcia being influenced by his student's sloppiness, which some critics have praised for its fire and energy. Several years ago Garcia seemed about to follow this path but we can all be happy that he did not and I hope he won't succumb to its wiles now.

"In sum, Garcia continues to move ever onward in the mastery of his subtle instrument, even though he is already far beyond any current practitioner of the art. His first student, Jorme, shows considerable promise and the restraining hand of his master may result in autarist second only to Garcia."

The image faded and the viewers began to stir, stretching their limbs and moving toward hors d'oeuvres and drinks.

"Don't pay too much attention to Elnor," Garcia said to Jorme. "He doesn't understand anything except technique."

Jorme looked up at Garcia, trying to hide the hurt in his eyes. "I'll show him, Garcia. Don't worry. I'll show him."

Chapter 18

When Shaara finally agreed to see Garcia, she was sitting in an armchair in her hospital suite, wrapped in a light blue robe. When he moved to embrace her, she pushed him away.

"Please, Garcia. There's still danger. My immune response hasn't fully recovered yet. Please. Sit down." She motioned to a seat on the far side of the room.

Garcia sat down slowly, looking at her. Her face was pale and she seemed somehow slighter, gaunt.

"Do I look that bad?" Her laughter was hollow.

"No. I just..."

She held up a hand. Garcia stopped, looking for the first time into her eyes, which seemed haunted with pain. "I know. I *do* look bad. Sometimes I think I'm not the same person." She looked away. "Father tried to warn me, but you won't know until you've been through it."

"Been through what?"

"The operation. The *second* operation. There's more to it than just implanting an artificial gland. The secretions of that gland, well, they have a very strong effect on the nervous system. It's been hell, Garcia, even with the drugs. It's taken longer for my body to adapt to the new hormones than anyone else has so far."

"Is it worth it then?"

"Yes!" Her laugh was brittle. "Oh, God, Garcia, there were times in the past few weeks when I wished I was dead, when I begged them to kill me, do anything to stop the pain. There was nothing they could do. But now the worst of it is over and my life means that much more to me. It's a very precious thing now, and those days of pain are nothing compared to the centuries ahead." She leaned toward him then stopped herself. "And you too, Garcia. Please hurry. I've talked to father and you can begin today. There's a limousine waiting for you outside and they'll take you to the laboratory. It'll only take a short time and then in a few months we'll be together for eternity."

"I don't know..." The pain and fear behind her eyes seared Garcia deeply.

"Please, Garcia. For me?"

"I..." What could he say. What could he do? "I'll think about it."

"Please, Garcia. Talk to Father."

On the journey to Muenstretiger's estate Garcia contemplated his course of action. The recognition of the pain that Shaara had gone through frightened him: he had never known much of physical pain himself and he feared it deeply. His missing arm began to twinge and ache as it hadn't in years. Was immortality worth such a price? Shaara had an answer for that: a few days of pain certainly were worth an eternity of life. He had no reply to that. He finally settled on an ambiguous solution: he would undergo today's operation, the brief excision of part of his thymus gland. By itself, it wasn't a final irrevocable decision for immortality. When the time came for the second operation, months from now, he could make his final decision.

Muenstretiger greeted him in the same brown study where they had first talked. "Shaara tells me you have some doubts about the operation."

"I've decided to go through with it. I thought it out on the way over."

"Good." Muenstretiger laid a hand on his shoulder with a gentle ease that was reassuring. Dr. Gregg would be disappointed if he didn't have his promised victim today."

"But..."

Muenstretiger raised an eyebrow. "But what? What are your reservations, Garcia?"

"There's more to it than just a couple of operations, isn't there?"

"Of course. You're still not protected from diseases. All we've done is provide you with a system for replacing lost body cells, for maintaining youth, so to speak. What you do with that is up to you. You can sit back and grow fat, courting heart disease, or you can keep trim and fit."

"It just seems too easy, that this artificial gland would provide just the right balance of hormones or whatever."

Muenstretiger smiled. "Not really. The body has its own regulatory feedback systems and this gland is fashioned from part of your own tissue, in fact, from one of the major regulatory organs. Of course, we have to keep close tabs on it, especially in the beginning, to make sure it doesn't run out of control."

"Has that happened?"

"A couple of times."

"What do you do then?"

Muenstretiger's smile was wan. "Remove the gland and start all over again."

ം‹›ം

Dr. Gregg had Garcia lie down on an operating table while a male nurse slapped an anesthetic patch on his neck. "You will truly be immortal now, Garcia."

What about you, Dr. Gregg? Garcia thought and he was surprised when the doctor answered. "Me? Like most of those who developed this process, I too am immortal."

Of course. Garcia hadn't been aware he had spoken, and this time he managed to keep the thought to himself. One must have immortal technicians and scientists to guard the immortal wealthy and powerful and their immortal playthings. It made sense, it all...

...all what? Garcia tried to capture the thought but it had already sprouted wings and flown away. He reached harder for it, but that only widened the distance between him and it, and he quit reaching, feeling a deep loss. Whatever the thought had been, it was a profound and important truth, and he feared having to relearn it again someday at a high cost.

"Ah, you are back with us, Garcia?" Dr. Gregg's voice, still sounding as though he was amused at some private joke, broke into Garcia's reverie. Garcia started to get up but the doctor's hand on his right shoulder restrained him. "Not yet. Lie still for a few minutes yet. You'll be stiff for a little while. I made the incision through the left side of your neck. That way the muscles that control your right arm won't be affected."

"But..."

"Oh, I know. I'm not stupid. I know you need control of your left hand as well. Don't worry. You'll just be sore for a couple of days. You won't have lost any of your dexterity." The doctor released his grip on Garcia's shoulder. "You may sit up now if you want to."

Garcia did so. A knot of soreness sent spider tendrils of pain across his neck, through his shoulder, and up the back of his neck. He felt dizzy and weak.

"The chauffeur will take you back to your apartment." Garcia swung his legs over the edge of the operating table and sat there, head down, fighting the dizziness. "I couldn't help but spend a little time examining the work on your right shoulder. Excellent work, excellent. McLeod, of course, is a fine surgeon. You are very lucky."

"Yes. Yes, I am."

Chapter 19

Garcia wanted to take Jorme's mind off Elnor's criticism by suggesting the two of them go to The Welcome Machine with Shaara and Pentland LaCroix. But Shaara wasn't willing to leave her father's estate. "Why don't you all just come over here instead?" she suggested.

"I was just thinking of a night out on the town for all of us, some excitement to keep Jorme busy. I thought maybe we could go to The Welcome Machine, like we did before."

"I can't do it, Garcia."

"Why not?"

"Things are different now."

"Different? Different how?"

"You know."

"No, I don't know." Garcia struggled to get his voice back under control. "What are you talking about?"

"Can Jorme hear us?"

"No. He's in my workshop. He's a very understanding person and he respects others' privacy."

"Garcia, try to look at it my way. I'm immortal now and I just don't want to do anything that would endanger that."

"How is going out for a night on the town going to endanger your precious immortality?"

"I know it doesn't look that way to you, Garcia, from your viewpoint. It's rather limited, but you still don't see it."

"I don't think my viewpoint is limited."

"No, you wouldn't. I can understand that. After all, my own viewpoint was limited too, just a few short weeks ago. But things are different now. When you have your operation then you'll understand. I think you probably already are beginning to understand. Think: why should I endanger centuries of life for just a few brief hours of enjoyment? Especially when the enjoyment can come here."

"Is that all I am to you? Enjoyment?"

"No, darling. Don't be a fool." Her voice was soft and consoling but the words bit deep into Garcia. "I don't have to go out into the city and endanger myself when you can come here where we'll both be safe from accidents and risk."

"That's not going to help Jorme any."

"All right, darling. You go out and have your fun tonight. But please take care of yourself and don't do anything rash."

Garcia watched in frustration as her image faded. Was she right? Would he feel the same way when he himself was immortal? Frightened to leave the safe warm confines of the Muenstretiger estate, where surely he would be living? Suddenly he didn't want to go out with Jorme and Pentland tonight—he remembered the crushing maw of a rivercleaner closing on his arm years ago. Shaara was right — the world outside her safe little womb *was* dangerous. There were simple accidents and failures of equipment, and there was the ever-present danger of other people's tempers. Even his apartment, so dear and sacred to him, was more dangerous than Muestretiger's estate.

"Well?"

"What?" Garcia looked up at Jorme. "Oh. No, she's still not completely recovered. We'll have to go alone. Why don't you call Pentland?"

"Do you think... I mean... I thought it was going to be the four of us, and..."

"I'll find someone." Garcia grinned. "I haven't erased my little black book yet."

He looked around the room while Jorme talked to Pentland. If he were to marry Shaara, he would have to give all this up and move onto her father's estate; that much was clear. She wouldn't come to live with him; she was rooted there and wouldn't leave for anything less than a national catastrophe. He touched the fireplace and its controls — on second thought, he probably wouldn't have to leave any of this behind. It could all be transported to the estate without leaving anything behind. He might even be able to have a genuine fireplace with a genuine wood fire in it... if Shaara didn't think it too dangerous.

"Pentland wants to talk to you." Garcia raised a questioning eyebrow but Jorme just spread his hands in a gesture of ignorance.

Garcia walked over to the stage. "Hi. What's the matter?"

"Jorme tells me Shaara isn't going with us."

"You know how it is. She's just had an operation and all..."

"Yes. What is this mysterious operation? You've never talked about it."

"No, I haven't." Garcia chuckled nervously. "You know how I am. I really haven't the slightest idea what it was about."

Pentland looked at him oddly. "If it was Jorme, I'd want to know every detail I could."

"We're different people, Pentland."

She looked at him for a long moment. "Yes, we are."

Garcia looked at Jorme on the other side of the room, engrossed in his autar. Jorme looked up suddenly, smiled, then continued practicing. "Look, Pentland." Garcia's voice was low and intense. "Shaara's okay. She's home now. The important thing is to get Jorme to relax. He's taking Elnor's criticism much too seriously. That's why I wanted to go out tonight. You *will* go out with us to The Welcome Machine, won't you?"

"Just you, me, and Jorme?"

"I'll find someone else. I'm not married to Shaara yet."

"Yet, huh? Okay. I'll be waiting for you."

Chapter 20

They passed through the maw of The Welcome Machine and sat at one of the tables in the balcony, looking over its edge at the students and others below. Another *grilly* band was at work, this one without a distinguishing vocalist, and the youngsters were busy writhing away their frustrations on the dance floor.

"Why don't you and Pentland go down and dance?" Garcia thought the physical activity might help drain away some of Jorme's tensions.

Pentland looked at Garcia. "I wouldn't dare."

"She'd be mobbed," Jorme said.

"I'm sorry. I wasn't thinking."

"I'll dance with you." Mars Ruby stood up. "Garcia never dances and I *love* to dance."

Jorme looked at Garcia, who nodded his approval.

Pentland waited until Jorme and Mars Ruby were gone, then said, "She loves you, you know."

Garcia spread his hands in resignation. "Does she? I *don't* know, Pentland. I know she cares for me more than she cares for anyone else, but is that love?"

"If that isn't, what is?"

While Garcia pondered that, his thought processes seeming to be incredibly slow, Pentland took his hand. "You love Shaara, don't you?"

"Do I? I don't know. I guess so."

"You *guess* so? You're planning to marry her, aren't you?"

Stupefied, Garcia could only stare at her. Was he that transparent? "Do you women have some kind of a private hot line?" he asked at last.

Pentland laughed. "No. but you're not acting at all like the Garcia of old."

"You didn't *know* the Garcia of old."

"No, but I've heard enough about him. Anyway, even if I hadn't been able to guess, Mars Ruby would have told me." She looked down at the dance floor. "Look at them down there." Jorme and Mars Ruby were moving violently among the other violently-moving bodies, Mars Ruby's scarcely-covered breasts bobbing and jiggling. "I envy them, in a way, you know?" She looked back at Garcia, who continued to stare at the dancers. "I wanted to be rich and famous, but I didn't realize how much that restricted your movement, and your freedom. I can't go down there and relax; I can't dance without worrying about someone coming up to me. I can't just go where the urge takes me. I have no control over my life. It's like being in prison."

"A pretty lush prison," Garcia said softly.

"Yes, but a prison nonetheless. You know a little of what I'm talking about, don't you?" Garcia nodded. "And it won't be long before Jorme will too." They were both silent a moment. "Is it true that you really don't dance, or do you just say that to keep from getting mobbed down there?"

"No, it's true." Garcia's voice was quiet and musing. "There never seemed to be enough time to learn."

"No, I guess not. There's never enough time. Sometimes I wish I could live forever."

"You could, you know."

"What?"

Garcia turned away, looking down at the dance floor again, surprised at himself, his guard down. "Nothing." But Pentland continued to stare at him, her countenance stern, her eyes searching.

"Garcia?" Her voice was soft. "Do you know something I don't?"

Well, why not? He had to tell *some*one. He couldn't keep it to himself forever. He turned back to her, back to those merciless eyes. "I said, you *could* live forever."

"That's what I thought you said."

"Listen, Pentland, if I tell you the whole thing, will you promise to tell no one else? Not even Jorme?"

She started to laugh, then stopped, realizing how serious Garcia was. "Why shouldn't I?"

"Not to protect me. To protect Jorme."

"Don't you think he's capable of protecting himself?"

"Look, you know how vulnerable he is. This would only make things worse for him."

Pentland looked at him for a moment longer, then glanced down at the table. "You might be right. Will you let me make the decision myself? You tell me what it is you have to tell me and I'll decide whether or not Jorme should know."

It made sense to Garcia. In any case, the secret was out now, with a person who had not been selected yet for the immortals. Whether or not Pentland told Jorme, she would eventually tell someone else and it would be over. What would he tell Jorme then? And Bwire?

Pentland listened quietly to Garcia's story, occasionally asking a question for clarification, until he had told her everything he could remember.

"And you've held this inside you for months?" He nodded. "I don't envy you, Garcia."

"Will you tell Jorme?"

"No. You're right. Now's not the time for him to know. But I'll have to tell him eventually."

"What about anyone else?"

Her eyes were steel again. "No. I'll keep your precious little secret, Garcia."

"Don't be too hard on me."

"If I tell someone else, eventually Jorme will find out, and I don't want to do anything that will hurt him. But once he knows, the secret will be out, even if he says nothing."

Garcia nodded. "It's a frightening thought."

"You don't know how frightening. While you were gone, there were two riots down in the *barraque*. Once they get wind of this..." She stopped. There were no words to describe what would happen then, nor were any necessary.

"What are you two talking about?" Jorme entered the alcove and collapsed into his chair. His face was bright and shiny, and his breath came in heavy sighs. Mars Ruby's face was bright and shiny too, but she seemed in perfect control of her breath.

"I was telling him about the riots down in the *barraque* a couple of weeks ago..."

Chapter 21

"Garcia. I have a call from Renard."

"Tell him I'll call him back. I'm busy right now." Garcia was halfway through a checkout of his autar, his special arm inserted deep into its innards, "seeing" the circuits with the aid of that arm's sensing devices, picking out needle points of dust and carefully removing them, checking capacitances and resistances, replacing parts and chips that seemed about to fail.

After a short pause the supervisor said, "He says it's important."

"Damn!" Garcia checked a molecular fusion he had made the last time on a chip that had had a microfracture. It still seemed secure but he had his doubts. "Okay. I'll take it here."

"Garcia?" There was a strange edge to Renard's voice.

"I'm here."

"Turn on the holostage."

"I'm in my workshop." There was no stage in Garcia's workshop.

"Oh." Renard paused a moment. "Let me know when you've reached a breakpoint."

Garcia ran down the checklist in the repair arm's computer. He was slightly more than halfway done but he could pick it up at any time in the future. "Go ahead."

"You're sure?"

"I'm sure. Go ahead." Garcia was getting annoyed. First Renard had interrupted him in the middle of working on his autar, and now he was wasting time.

"Uh, I don't know how to tell you this, Garcia, but... well, Bwire died thirty minutes ago."

Garcia stared at the autar in front of him, an uncomfortable warmth creeping up his chest. Although he wasn't crying, his eyes suddenly seemed hot. Even though he had been expecting it for such a long time, it still hurt. No more to know Bwire's exasperating peregrinations, to know his waspish tongue, to bask in the warmth of his rare praise. Somehow, he had never really believed that Bwire would die, that he would just slowly wither away as he had for the past few years, always there, always subtly guiding Garcia with his sarcasm. If it hadn't been for Bwire...

"Garcia?"

"Yes." Garcia cleared his throat. "I heard you, Renard. Thank you. Thank you very much."

"Is there anything I can do?"

"I don't know. I can't think of anything right now. I guess I'm not thinking too clearly."

"Well, don't worry about it. I'll take care of everything. I'll send the message and..."

"No!" Garcia's sharp response cut Renard off in mid-sentence. "I'll handle everything."

"Look, Garcia, there's no need to..."

"Renard," Garcia said softly, "Bwire was like a father to me. This is a private personal thing, okay?"

"Sure, Garcia. Sure."

Garcia sat in his workshop for a long moment, unseeing, his thoughts and emotions a chaotic jumble. Finally, he asked the supervisor to connect him with Bwire's apartment but the number had already been disconnected. While he tried to figure out what to do next, Jorme called. He already had the information Garcia wanted.

"His daughter's going to take care of everything, Garcia. Did you know he had a daughter?"

"Yes." Bwire talked of her less and less as he had grown old. Garcia had met her only once. She must be nearly fifty now, Garcia thought, maybe older, but he didn't really know.

"I didn't. It's hard to think of Bwire having children."

Bwire had hundreds of children, Garcia thought, and he and Jorme were only two of them. But he was the favorite, he thought, jealously guarding that distinction.

"The cremation will be tomorrow."

So soon. So soon. Hardly cold and stiff, he would be reduced to elements and released. Would the soul fly upward and be consumed in the flames, never to know an immortality of any kind. The soul. Garcia had never known religion except at a distance, hearing of the dreams of immortality and a better life that waited after death for the workers in the *barraque*. He had never believed in the soul, in an afterlife, or in a reincarnation, but now he fervently wanted to believe, for Bwire, if not for himself. It seemed unfair that so good a man as Bwire should just cease to be, without leaving anything behind but a few memories, traces of acetylcholine in a few brains that in their time would cease to be as well, until the only thing that remained of Bwire would be a few words in a computer somewhere, a few on-and-off bits to be resurrected occasionally by some historian.

There had to be more. It just wasn't right; it wasn't fair. But who had ever told Garcia the world was fair?

He contacted Bwire's daughter, who told him Bwire had requested he play a short Rujula requiem at the funeral. "You don't have to be here personally, of course. There's a holostage at the crematorium."

"I'll be there personally." He paused, uncertain how to mention this. "The last time I saw Bwire, he asked me to complete a composition for him."

"He left a number of things to you. Most of them are of no use to us, music, and things like that."

And that was that. He would go to the funeral tomorrow, play the Rujula requiem for people who wouldn't appreciate it, for a man who would appreciate it but who wouldn't be able to hear it, who wouldn't be able to give him a critical appraisal when it was complete. It would be just an empty gesture for the empty husk of a man.

Chapter 22

Jorme and Pentland were already there when Garcia arrived for Bwire's funeral. Bwire's daughter and her children were also there along with several others whom Garcia didn't know, and a handful of Bwire's pupils and colleagues.

He went through the ordeal of greeting the family, forgetting names as quickly as they were mentioned, and went over to look at his mentor, lying in a stasis field on a block of plastigranite. Bwire was wearing his favorite blue robe, its folds neater and more orderly than ever they had appeared in life. The lines and creases of his face were relaxed and the hands that had become claws were at peace by his side. There was no hint of the sarcasm and the biting tongue, only a sad old man who had come to the end of his road.

"Garcia?" A small man with a fringe of red whiskers was at his side. The man introduced himself as a lawyer, the executor of Bwire's estate. He handed Garcia a large package. "He wanted you to have these. There's some personal things, and a note."

"Thank you."

"He also wanted you to have one of his autars."

"The best one," Bwire's daughter said in a bitter tone. "You'd think he would be more thoughtful of his family, wouldn't you, Garcia? I'm sure you understand..."

"Understand?"

"That autar is worth a great deal.

"I see." It seemed obscene to be talking like this in front of Bwire's corpse. Garcia's voice took on an edge of steel. "You want me to refuse my claim to the instrument."

"Well, it's the only honorable..."

"Bwire wanted me to have that instrument. He had his good and just reasons, I'm sure. You know very little about music, even though you're his daughter. That instrument, one of the finest in the world, could wind up in anybody's hands, if you were to have your way."

"Well, of course I'd be careful."

"I *want* that instrument. In addition to its being so valuable, it meant a great deal personally to Bwire and hence to me as well."

The woman looked at Garcia angrily. "I thought you'd be more understanding than *that*." She started to turn away.

"I'll have it appraised and send you its value," Garcia said bitterly, his sorrow overwhelmed by the feeling of being soiled by this contact with Bwire's daughter. He turned to the lawyer. "You'll have it sent to me?"

"Of course."

Sullenly he played the Bujula requiem, trying to lose himself in the music and his last homage to Bwire, but the day now had a bitter taste to it. He left as soon as he was done, the tension in his wake being swept by the good-natured Jorme and the level-headed Pentland.

"What did Bwire leave you?" Jorme asked. "In the envelope."

"Just some papers. He wanted me to finish one of his compositions."

"That's great! You'd be an incredible composer."

Garcia looked at his pupil. "Just because I've mastered one instrument doesn't mean I can compose music. It's something else entirely."

"But surely the two skills would complement each other?" Pentland said.

"If you've got both of them. I don't."

"Are you sure?"

Garcia grunted. "I took a composing class at the conservatory. I didn't do very well in it. Bwire knew it."

They went to Garcia's apartment, where Garcia poured some wine and put on a holocube of one of Bwire's performances, when he was still young, younger than Garcia was now.

The lines of old age were gone. One could not even guess where they might appear on that sharply handsome face with the straight nose that would turn into a parody of a cruel beak with age. The gray and brittle hair was dark and sleek, full of body. The eyes that were so piercing and the smile that was so full of bite were now gentle and misted, no trace of sarcasm present. And the hands... the gnarled, twisted claws were supple and moved with a life of their own across the strings of the instrument, darting rapidly to the controls to change the program as the flow of the music altered. Bwire had never mastered control of his little finger the way Garcia had, needing the strength of two fingers to change the settings but, at his best, when this tape had been recorded, Bwire had a speed that Garcia had never quite matched.

"He was... good, wasn't he?" Pentland's voice was oddly choked. Garcia wondered whether she was somehow touched by Bwire's death, through him and Jorme, or by the music to which they were listening. He was pleased that she didn't say *great*, or some other superfluous word. *Good* was an understatement, but it fit Bwire more elegantly than some more grandiose word.

"He was very good," Garcia said quietly.

"I've seen some of his cubes, but I don't think I've ever seen this one."

"It's a private recording. There aren't many copies of it around."

There was a smattering of applause; it had been a very small and select audience. Bwire looked out of the holostage directly at Garcia, a strange saintly smile on his face, and Garcia felt tears come to his eyes. Then the master looked down at his instrument, the very instrument that now belonged to Garcia, and began playing again.

Garcia opened the packet on his lap. As he had expected, there were quite a few sheets of music, annotated in Bwire's careful spidery hand. On top was a short note, written in that same spidery script, shaky yet firm:

Garcia—When you read this, I shall be dead, probably by several days. It doesn't matter. I've led a good and enjoyable life, even exciting at times, and the best parts are over. I am not "going gentle into that good night," as the phrase has it— I intend the give Old Man Death a good thrashing when I meet him. Garcia smiled. *You were the best of my pupils, not despite your recalcitrance and stubbornness, but because of it. I learned more from you than from all the rest of my students put together. It is one reason why I suggested you take a student: I suspect one learns more from teaching than from being taught.*

You have always placed too much emphasis on your playing. It has become your entire life and that has placed restrictions on you which you do not even suspect. I cried for you, and with you, over the death of Stella Blue but at the same time I was glad for you, because it was a step forward, out of your shell.

Now it is time for the next step. I wish I could be here to share it with you but perhaps it is my own death that will in-

stigate your taking it. Perhaps not. Perhaps I put too much emphasis on my own influence on you.

"No." Garcia almost choked on the syllable. Jorme looked over at him with a questioning look and Pentland laid a cool hand on his.

"You loved him, didn't you?"

Garcia nodded, unwilling to trust his voice.

There is something growing inside you, a restlessness. I don't know its exact cause but please don't disregard it. Follow it, Garcia. It may be hard at times but you will not regret it. Reach, strive. Go over the edge.

Good luck, my friend and my finest pupil. I have faith in you.

Garcia looked up from the note, only barely aware of Jorme and Pentland, seeing only that falsely substantial image of a man he barely remembered, young and full of life, playing his autar as though his life depended on it.

Chapter 23

The holostage was silent; Bwire was back in his cube. The false logs in Garcia's fireplace popped and crackled. The three of them were slightly tipsy from the wine; Garcia knew they would all feel its effects in the morning.

"Did you know those other people at the funeral?" Pentland asked.

"Some of them." Garcia's voice was soft. "There were several people there from the conservatory, students of Bwire's, some of my classmates."

"You hardly talked to them."

"We weren't friends. I didn't have many friends back then."

Pentland touched him on the arm. "You've got friends now."

Jorme wandered around the room, half drunk, looking at the false books in the bookcases, peering into gargoyled corners, staring at the pseudo-leather furniture. For a time he had toyed with his autar, playing aimless random tunes—even drunk, he was too good a musician to play something with no musical value. Now he stood in front of one of the pseudo-bookcases, his fingers probing its side.

"Hey, Garcia, something's wrong here. I think your bookcase is falling apart."

"That's the emergency exit."

"Emergency exit?"

"If there's a power failure or something like that and the elevators quit working, that kind of thing."

"No kidding? How does it work??"

"You have to operate it manually." Garcia walked over to the fireplace. A small lever disguised as a poker came down slowly and the bookcase swiveled to reveal an unadorned and functional door behind it.

"Where does it lead?"

"To a stairway."

Jorme opened the door and walked out onto a naked cement landing. The stark unfinished functional quality of the emergency exit contrasted sharply with the opulence of Garcia's apartment. The cement was rough to the touch, feeling almost as though it could break the skin at the tips of one's fingers as Jorme ran his over it. Stairways led from the platform, one up and one down.

"That one goes all the way down to the ground floor?"

"It's supposed to. I have no desire to find out, however, unless it becomes absolutely necessary."

"And that one?" Jorme pointed to the stairway going up.

"To the apartments above mine, I would suppose."

"And the roof?"

"Perhaps."

Jorme started up the stairway. "Let's find out. You're not far from the top, are you?"

Garcia walked to the doorway. "Not so fast. What do you want to go up there for? You won't see anything you can't see from my workshop."

"Come on, Garcia. Just for the hell of it. What do you say? Pentland?"

The actress looked at Garcia hopelessly. Well, why not? Perhaps this was what Bwire had in mind. The youthfulness and the playfulness of Jorme, his boyishness, was something Garcia had never known. He had always been a serious solitary youth, a bit afraid of other children, unable to join in their play. It seemed to come naturally to other people, to Jorme, to Justin, to Mars Ruby, even to Pentland and Shaara; but Garcia had to work at it and learn it.

"Okay. Let's go."

Four flights later, the stairway ended at a doorway. Jorme tried the door, but it wouldn't open.

"It's probably the top apartment and it certainly wouldn't open for us," Garcia said.

"You try."

Garcia tried to open the door but had no better success than Jorme had had.

"There's a lock over here." Pentland pointed to the small space on the door frame. "Why don't you try that?"

Garcia pressed his thumb against the space and the door swung open smoothly, letting in a small cool evening breeze, the faint scent of smoke and oil, and whispers of distant sounds. They hesitantly entered a small dusty room full of machinery at the top of the building. Even as they stood there, the machinery began to whine. "That must be the elevator," Jorme said.

Garcia wanted to get as far away from it as possible, his heart suddenly pumping wildly as the thought of how many times he had trusted his body and his life to that fragile, whining piece of machinery. Machines died too, just like men, and they often took men with them when they did.

"Look!" Pentland had wiped away a clear space on one of the dusty windows in the shed. "It's beautiful!"

Through the small clear space they could see the lights of the city spread out before them, as they could be seen from Garcia's workroom. The young lovers pressed against the glass, looking out.

"Don't you want to see, Garcia?"

"I can see just as good a view from the comfort of my workroom."

Jorme was prowling around again and suddenly he opened a door Garcia hadn't been aware of, letting the breeze that had circulated softly in the shed become a blast of spring wind lifting dust and scattering papers, spreading them randomly throughout the tiny shed. The small building was suddenly full of sound, the wind like a synthesizer, the underlying sounds of the city running a faint counterpoint.

"My God!" The awe in Jorme's voice brought Garcia reluctantly over to his side, where Pentland had already rushed when Jorme had opened the door.

The city was now clearly visible all around them, a panoramic view that dwarfed the limited one from Garcia's workshop. All the strings of light seemed to converge on this building, like spokes in a wheel, although Garcia knew it was only an illusion, like the illusion that the Earth was the center of the universe. Across the spokes, other rays of light crossed and recrossed, moving out in waves of light from the building to the distant horizon, until they disappeared in the distance. The jewels of the city glowed and glittered all around them. The wind blew viciously across the top of the building, carrying traces of smoke and remnants of odd perfumes, intermingled smells of distant factories and nearby buildings. Although the top of the building had been swept clean by the wind, the dust and rubbish inside the small structure at the top of the elevator shaft was now available for the wind to play with and it swirled and mixed around the little construction gleefully, moving dust out into the night air and blowing papers into the far distance.

"It's beautiful!" Pentland moved out onto the roof of the building.

"Be careful." Garcia was fearful of going out any further onto the roof than the safe confines of the doorway.

"Don't worry."

"Is the view from your workshop as good as this?" Jorme asked.

"No. But it's safer." And the roar of the city was unheard there, its rhythms like a fast-beating heart unfelt.

"What's that?" Pentland pointed to an actinic glare that pierced the sky's darkness to the south, some distance away.

"That must be one of the shuttles going up to the starship," Jorme said. "The launching ground is down there on the peninsula."

The two lovers walked out onto the roof, moving fearlessly closer to the edge, while Garcia stayed near the elevator housing, fear molten inside his chest. He became more acutely aware of the steady hum and rhythm underneath the singing of the wind as its voice rose and fell, sometimes so loud it seemed to contain all the sounds of the world, then falling to a faint susurrus under which the steady hum and rhythm of the city could be heard, the distant call of a muted foghorn or other warning device, the faint grinding of the river cleaners.

"Don't go too near the edge," he shouted out. "Be careful! This wind could blow you right off."

"Don't worry." Pentland's voice was almost carried away by the wind. Her dark hair blew wildly in the wind, visible only by the flickering glitter light that it reflected in prismatic shards.

When they finally returned to the shed, her face was alive and aglow, as was Jorme's. The effect of the beauty of the scene, of the wind, made them more alive, fresh, and vibrant than Garcia himself had ever been, more so perhaps than he had ever seen anyone look before.

Chapter 24

Garcia stared at the notes in front of him but he didn't really see them. His mind wandered as he tried to follow Bwire's music but he wasn't yet aware his concentration was gone. Looking at the key change in the middle of the second movement, he had begun daydreaming about the possibility of keying in a fret change at that point, so that the new key would use natural harmonies rather than the tempered scale. The problem with keying in the change was the performer would then be unable to perform while the change was taking place. Relying on the computer to maintain melodic flow was repugnant to Garcia. If there were some way to maintain a balance during the key change, sliding with the flow...

He had spent fifteen minutes playing with key changes, trying to find ways to maintain melodic flow during the change but not succeeding. The computer was too fast for him, and his pressure on the keyboard during the change modified the speed of the key change in an unpredictable manner.

While the tension of the strings could be varied one by one through programming, it was not possible to change the fret pattern except across the whole keyboard. Still, there was no reason why it had to be that way. It was just that no one had ever thought of changing one fret at a time before. He would call Althor Burn to see if a special autar could be made which would allow modular changes to the fret pattern. And while he was at it, why not allow the speed of the changes to be determined by the performer instead of always at a fixed speed?

He looked at the music, seeing it again for the first time in minutes. There was no sense in working further on the concerto until he had talked to Althor Burn, indeed, not until he had such an autar in his hands, and that would take months.

Months. Months from now, he would be immortal. Would it matter then? Yes, he knew it would. He would no longer be thinking in terms of leaving behind something besides a few ephemeral cubed performances. What did it matter what modifications and improvements he made to the instrument? What did it matter whether or not he left behind his own concertos and compositions? After a couple of hundred years, much less a thousand, would it matter to him?

As if in answer to his thoughts, Shaara chose this moment to call him. "Why don't you move here so we can be together again?" she suggested. "I haven't seen you in so long."

"I will. Don't worry. But I can't leave here just yet."

"Why not? We can reconstruct your apartment without any trouble. I worry about you, Garcia. So much could happen to you. It would be such a tragedy if something were to happen to you when you were so close to immortality."

"Don't worry. I can take care of myself. And it's not nearly as dangerous out here as you think."

"That's what you say now. When you're immortal, you'll realize how precious your life is and how foolish it is to endanger it in silly ways..."

As she talked, Garcia thought about the night before, when he had stood on the roof with Pentland and Jorme. They had not been afraid of going out on the roof, exposing themselves to the wind and to danger, however slight, while he had cowered against the elevator housing. They had been so alive when they had returned, while he had felt half-dead with fear. If he had not had immortality dangling in front of him like a carrot, would he have joined them? Would he have known their exhilaration, the sharp knife-edge of daring the inevitable, of spitting in the face of the grave?

"Darling?"

"I'm sorry. What did you say?"

"Father's giving a small party tomorrow night. All the immortals will be there and we'd like you to come."

"Of course."

"The way things are going, it may be the last time all the immortals will be able to gather together in one place."

"How's that?"

"There'll be too many of us soon. Besides, it wouldn't be a good idea for all of us to gather at one time. We'd all be too vulnerable. It would be more than a tragedy, it would be a disaster, if all the immortals were destroyed."

"Yes, I suppose it would be."

"So I'll see you tomorrow night?"

"Of course."

"I can hardly wait, Garcia."

"Neither can I." Why then did he feel so reluctant, why did the prospect seem a dreary one?

"And please think about moving out here as soon as possible."

He looked again at Bwire's half-finished composition. Would any of the people at the party understand anything about it?

Chapter 25

One of Muenstretiger's chauffeurs picked Garcia up and drove him through the streets in a car that seemed more armored tank than limousine. Most of the same people were there who had been at the previous party, but Jack Orion was notably absent. Shaara's "small party" included close to one hundred people.

"Are all the people here immortal?" he asked Shaara.

"Most of them. Some of them have yet to take the treatment and others, like my father, are already too old for it. But their sons and daughters have, or will."

Garcia realized that, although his own name and face were better known and more easily recognized than any of the other immortals and immortals-to-be, it was they who really controlled things. He was just a pawn, the court jester to Muenstretiger's court, his captured pet monkey, a prize to display as he would a painting by an old master or a sculpture or a rare recording or a fine wine.

"Where's Dr. Gregg?"

"This party is just for the immortals."

"But hasn't he taken the operation?"

"It's not the same thing. They are..." She paused, searching for the appropriate word. "...technicians. They wouldn't be interested in people like us."

Garcia remembered their first meeting, when she had described herself apologetically as a social butterfly. Now she seemed to revel in her position; she was in her element, and he was a fish out of water.

Mont'Illiano placed a friendly hand on Garcia's shoulder. "It's good to see you again. A shame you didn't bring your autar. I understand you're going to join us."

"I'm thinking about it, yes," Garcia said slowly.

"Good! We need someone here besides all these old stodgy people without any talent except for making money."

"Monty!" Shaara admonished him.

"Well, it's true. That's all *I* do: just charm money out of our stockholders." He turned back to Garcia. "I understand one of your teachers died recently, ah..."

"Bwire."

"Yes. He supposedly was the finest autarist of his day."

"I learned a great deal from him."

"All the more reason why you should complete your treatment as soon as possible. Artists like you are rare; you're national treasures and should be treated as such."

"Put in dusty cabinets and taken out on holidays?" Garcia had tried to make the tone of his voice light but there was a trace of bitterness there nonetheless.

Mont'Illiano looked at his sharply. "No, that's not what I meant. But it *is* true that you'd have to curtail your performance schedule drastically. It's one thing for an ephemeral person to do as much as he can in the short time he's allowed, but now we're freed from those restrictions and we must take the long view."

"I'm afraid I haven't gotten used to thinking in those terms."

"None of us have yet. We're still learning. But we can afford to go cautiously, one step at a time."

And what would that mean for the electromotive industry, the communications industry, the pharmaceutical industry? A slow appraisal, perhaps centuries in length, of any developments, with the emphasis on those developments that would benefit the immortals, such as a rejuvenation for those who had been in their late years when the discovery was made. Garcia felt as if he were on the edge of an important revelation but he had no idea yet what it might be.

"Have you met President Quan?" Mont'Illiano introduced Garcia to a small man with a nervous energy that seemed out of place among these serene captains and ladies of industry.

"I believe we are the only non-immortals here," he said to Garcia.

"What about the servants?"

"Oh yes. I forgot about them."

"Do they know about the process?"

"Oh no. I'm sure Muenstretiger hasn't informed them about it. After all, we have to inform the public about this very quietly. There isn't enough expertise and equipment yet to offer it immediately to any but a small portion of the people. You can imagine the consequences if the information were to leak out to the public."

Garcia could, and he wondered how much longer the secret could be kept. The people at this "small party" talked openly and freely to each other about their status, ignoring the servants as though they weren't even there. If they hadn't known about the immortality process before this evening, surely some of them knew about it now. Some would keep their own counsel, perhaps offering their silence to Muenstretiger in return for the operation, but not all of them.

"Are you planning on another trip to The Welcome Machine?" he asked Mont'Illiano.

"Oh, no." Mont'Illiano's laughter seemed hollow. "Things are different now, you know. I have to take care of myself now. You understand, don't you?"

Garcia nodded, thinking that maybe he understood more than Mont'Illiano himself did.

Chapter 26

"Garcia, I want to talk to you." There was an edge to Jack Orion's words and an intensity to his expression that Garcia had never seen before.

"Go ahead. Talk."

"I don't know if I should over this line. Maybe I should come over in person."

"Orion, I'm a busy man. Tell me what it is you want, or don't bother."

Orion hesitated, his face a mask of indecision. "All right. Listen, are you still seeing Shaara Muenstretiger?"

"What do your spies tell you?"

"Cut it out, Garcia." Orion was exasperated, and Garcia realized he was on the edge of losing control. His face was haggard and its lines and wrinkles were emphasized by his weariness. "We're both on the same side."

"All right, all right. Yes, I'm still seeing her. If you must know, we're thinking of getting married." There. It was out, a bit to Garcia's own surprise.

But not to Orion's. "I was afraid of that," he said wearily. "Listen, I've found out what I was looking for and I think you should know too, just... just in case."

"Just in case of what?"

"Never mind." Orion took a deep breath and the old confidence and brashness returned. "I've been hearing lots of ugly rumors lately and I'm pretty sure they're true. I've tracked them down and I trust my informants. It all holds together." Garcia waited. "Muenstretiger has discovered a way to make people immortal and he and the rest of the rich people are now immortal, including Shaara."

"That's absurd." Even if Jack Orion's facts were slightly askew, the basic fact was true. But Garcia would never admit it to Orion.

Orion peered at Garcia, trying to pierce his bluff. "You don't know anything about this?"

"How could I?"

"How could you? You're thinking of marrying Shaara, you've been to several of their parties, one where immortality was mentioned openly among the guests. Garcia, how could you *not* know?"

Garcia let out a weary breath. "Orion, you've had more to do with these people than I have, and how long has it taken you to find this out? I'm just a toy to them, a musician, an entertainer."

Orion sat back, obviously wanting to believe Garcia but still uncertain. "In any case, the news is out, and I'm going to blow it sky high this evening. There's nothing they can do to stop me. But I'm disappointed in you, Garcia; I had hoped for better things from you."

"I'm sorry. I don't live my life for your approval, Orion. I'm a musician, a performer, and that's what my life revolves around. Everything else is secondary."

"There are more important things to life than music."

"So they tell me." Garcia made no attempt to keep the sarcastic edge out of his voice.

Jack Orion sat on the holostage, his head nodding slowly as he looked at Garcia. "Someday, Garcia, someday..." And he broke the connection.

Garcia sat there, still watching the stage as though Orion were still on it. So the commentator finally knew. It wasn't surprising; the surprising part was that it had taken him so long to find out. Immortality wasn't something you could keep a secret for very long. And now what would happen? Orion would record his commentary immediately and, in a very short time, the world would know, high and low, small and great. And Garcia would have to face his friends and tell them that he was one of the elect, and they were not.

"Supervisor. Get me Mont'Illiano's office at Metropolitan."

A few seconds later a strange slender young man appeared on Garcia's holostage. "Can I help you?"

"I'd like to talk to Mont'Illiano."

"He's busy right now. I can take a message for him."

"I need to talk to him right now. This is important."

"I'm sorry. I can't do that. If you'll leave a message, he will call you right back."

Garcia angrily broke the connection. One of *them*? No, he wasn't part of Mont'Illiano's society, any more than he was part of Jack Orion's imaginary romantically-tinged *barraquistes*. He was himself, Garcia, and no one else. If he belonged to any group, it was that of musicians, but he could only call a handful of them his friends—Bwire, Jorme, Justin Mead. Who else? Who else, indeed?

Should he call Shaara? No, leave her out of this, leave them all out of this. But he was alone—he needed the advice of Bwire but that advice was forever beyond him. He paced the apartment, solitude bearing on him like the merciless rhythm of *Bolero*, Perhaps... perhaps...

"Supe, try to get Jorme for me."

But when Jorme appeared on his holostage, Garcia didn't know what to say, how to tell Jorme what he wanted and needed. "Are you busy tonight?" he asked at last. "I'd like to just go out for a couple of hours." Jorme was hesitant. "What's the matter? Did you and Pentland have something planned for tonight?"

"No. No. she's over at Metropolitan tonight, working. But... I'm afraid I don't understand, Garcia. I mean, what did you want to do?"

Garcia smiled, realizing how out of character it was for him to suggest a night out on the town. "I'm not sure I can explain it, Jorme. I just needed to get out of here and do something with some friends and I thought of you and Justin. Do you mind?"

"No. Sure. Of course not."

Justin was delighted with the idea and they met him at The Welcome Machine shortly after dusk. It was too early for any of the real action; it was strictly *ordinary* time, music to fill the souls and titillate the minds of young straights and new-comers looking for the heart of the city. The real grotesquerie would not begin for hours. Jorme didn't seem to mind but Justin was restless.

"Let's go down to the *barraque*."

"I don't know." Garcia was hesitant, a bit fearful and uncertain.

"Look. This may be your last night on the town before you get married. Then that'll be the end of that. You don't know what it's like."

Garcia smiled. "Yes. I've noticed how you never get out at all these days."

Justin laughed. "Touché." He held his hands up in a gesture of defeat. "But it will be a while before the novelty wears off. What about it, Jorme? Want to go down to the *barraque*?" Jorme shrugged his shoulders. "We can go down and see Garcia's old haunts. What was the name of that place where you met Stella Blue?"

"The Row Jimmy."

"Right. Come on. We can come back here later."

The electrocab left them off at street level, several levels above the *barraque*, and they descended by the old stone wall, down one of the few lighted stairways remaining, to the noise and commotion of the *barraque* night.

Although the *barraque* had many old street lights, most of them were shattered and broken, and the three musicians walked in shadow. A riverfront portion of town, it had known its up and downs, prosperity, decay, the rise back to being an attraction where craft shops and expensive restaurants were found, another decay, a time of expensive gambling casinos that naturally ran down to vice and corruption, and so on, swinging back and forth. It was on the rise again: in a few years it would probably be the chic spot in which to live and carouse. Right now, however, figures moved through the shadows, some stumbling and reeling. From the bars and clubs, the music was often drowned out by laughter and loud conversation, sometimes by angry shouts and cries.

Most of the buildings were constructed of centuries' old brick, the crumbling mortar patched and shored dozens of times in thousands of places. The pavement of the streets was cracked and holed, pitted and scarred.

If there were few street lights to provide illumination, there was some light that streamed out of the establishments, although many kept a dim glow for atmosphere, and for illegal transactions.

The Row Jimmy was gone. Its windows were broken, and there were a couple of rotting boards hammered across its closed door, as if to stop anyone who didn't want to enter through the windows. Inside was darkness — the place might be empty or it might harbor a dozen thugs; it was impossible to tell.

"The famous Row Jimmy," Garcia said sardonically. "Can I buy you boys a drink?"

"No respect for history," Justin said.

They walked slowly down the cracked street. In other bars, heavy-set men in grimy clothes talked and drank. Nearly every bar had a stopgo table, some of them broken. Nearly every third bar had a *grilly* band, some worse, some better, than the one Garcia had heard at The Welcome Machine.

They chose a bar that was quieter than the others. The twenty or so people in it morosely, and bitterly, nursed their drinks. The bandstand in the far corner apparently had not been used in quite some time: its stage was littered with plaster, dust, and trash. The two chairs on it were broken and mangled; the microphone stand that rose from the base was without a microphone.

"Welcome to the *barraque*," Garcia said to Jorme as they sat down at a table chosen at random from the many empty tables in the bar.

"I'll get our drinks,." Justin headed over to the bar.

"I've *been* to the *barraque* before many times." Jorme's voice indicated the insult he felt at Garcia's patronizing tone. "I know what it's like."

"Probably better than I do."

"Perhaps."

Justin returned with their drinks. "I'm not sure it was a good idea to choose this place," he said. "After all, there must be some reason why there's so few customers here while there's so many in the other bars."

Garcia tasted his drink. "What does it matter?"

"Maybe it's because nothing's happening here," Jorme said. "Everyone's going to the bars where something's happening."

"Great!" Justin stared at them. "We go out for a night on the town and pick the bar where nothing's happening."

"Garcia," a guttural voice said as a heavy hand fell on Garcia's shoulder. He turned around to see Auguste, the gorilla who had been working at the Row Jimmy when Garcia had first met Stella Blue. "You play?" Auguste gestured toward the dusty bandstand.

"I can't. I don't have my autar with me. You work here now, Augie?"

"Yuh. Come?" Augie started toward a door at the back of the bar and Garcia got up to follow him.

"Where are you going?" Jorme asked.

"Don't worry. Augie's okay. He used to take care of me, back when I hung around here years ago."

In the dingy stockroom, piled high with cases of liquor and other supplies, Augie led Garcia to a battered old guitar, half its strings gone, and the others too stiff with time to play.

"You play?" Augie repeated.

"I can't play this, Augie. The strings are no good."

"I fix maybe. You wait."

While waiting for the gorilla to return, Garcia looked around the storeroom. Small animals rustled in the dark back corners and something chattered overhead. He felt shivers go up his spine as he thought of someone spending his entire life in a place like this. Who would want to be immortal then?

Augie returned with the bar's owner, a small man with a lined face, looking every bit the hustler he was. "Garcia? Are you really Garcia? Augie says you want to play."

"No. *Augie* wants me to play. But I can't play this." Garcia held up the guitar.

"But you *will* play?" the owner asked eagerly. "I have strings for it."

Garcia shrugged. "Sure. Why not?"

The owner hesitated a moment then said, "I have an autar too, if you'd like to play that instead. It's not a very good one, of course, but..."

"Let me see it."

When the owner hurried off to fetch his autar and the guitar strings, Garcia went back to the table with the battered guitar.

"What the hell is *that*?" Jorme asked.

"A guitar. What does it look like?"

"I don't know. Don't tell me you're going to try to play it."

"I might." Garcia began stripping off the remaining strings. A couple of the other customers looked over in lackadaisical interest. He wiped off the plaster and dust that covered its surface. The guitar was not a good one—its plastic body was cracked in several places, and the neck was beginning to separate from the body. Still, it looked playable.

The owner returned with the strings and his autar. He was right—it was one of the cheapest autars around, with barely a 12K memory. It was autars like this that made amateurs give up. Even when Garcia keyed the tuning button, the autar still wasn't in tune. He had to tune it manually, not an easy job on an instrument that wasn't meant for manual tuning.

"Think you can play this thing?" he asked Jorme.

The youngster looked at it doubtfully. "I suppose so. But I don't know if I want to."

"Did you bring your flute with you?" he asked Justin.

"Of course." Justin took the flute out of his jacket pocket and began assembling it, while Jorme played the autar softly and Garcia began restringing the guitar. Augie stood over them, watching eagerly.

"You play now?" he asked when Garcia had finished restringing the guitar.

"We'll try."

"Wait." The gorilla went into the back room again, returning with a broom. He swept off the stage, threw the broken chairs off it, and picked up three new ones from the tables. He looked ruefully at the empty microphone stand. "Do you need?" he asked as the three musicians came up to the stage.

"No. That's all right, Augie. We don't need it."

Augie smiled one of his rare smiles. "You like?"

"It's great, Augie." He patted the gorilla on the back. "Everything's fine."

"Augie fix good."

"Some night on the town," Justin said.

"How are you at *grilly*?" Garcia asked Jorme.

"Not much better than those guys at The Welcome Machine. I used to listen to it a lot but I never played much of it."

"No time like the present to learn. You'll have to lead. I don't think you could do much following with that instrument."

They started off with some soft classical music, easily accessible to the *barraquistes*, with a steady rhythm from the autar, Garcia and Justin running harmonies around Jorme's melodic line. Several times he and Justin clashed, sometimes they chose the same harmony line, but no one else in the bar was aware of it.

As they played, Garcia became aware of the audience in the bar muttering his name over and over again. "Garcia!" "What's he doing here?" "That's his student. What's his name?" And the name of Stella Blue also surfaced and then went down, coming up again. It was a strange bifurcation of his energies and concentration, one that was present in his usual concerts but was enhanced in the small bar until it reached a peak he hadn't known since his brief span as a guitarist at the Row Jimmy: he was two people, at once aware of the audience and their reaction to his music, and at the same time caught up in the music itself and pushing it to its limits. The two streams augmented each other—as the audience reacted to the music, Garcia became more involved with it, and their reaction became stronger.

It was no longer three musicians trying to find one another. He had played often enough with Jorme and Justin separately to understand them and to have a good idea where each of them would go next in their melodic structures. Justin and Jorme still had to learn to work with each other, but they were professionals enough to do it well, if unspectacularly. A few words were all that was necessary: "Radcliffe's *Goldfinch*" from Garcia, and Jorme slowed down the tempo as Garcia made the change from simple exercises to the brief sonata; "Plastic Mother," Justin said (unexpected from him since he wasn't a *grilly* enthusiast), and Garcia strummed rhythm as the flute player went into the stratosphere; "Norwegian Wood" from Jorme, and he took the lead on the old folk tune.

Outside, in the *barraque*, the wave of information went out like the ripples from a rock thrown into the river: "Garcia's back!" "He's at Wood's Hole." The quiet bar became jammed, people shouting their favorite songs, screaming. A woman, her face horribly disfigured, moved to the front of the crowd as Justin, Jorme, and Garcia started to play "Concrete Lover." She began singing, in a clear liquid voice that contained all the pain and ache of the *barraque*:

"Concrete lover, hard as a rock,
Brittle as ice, a key with no lock."

As she moved toward the stage, Augie moved to block her from the platform. Garcia gestured him away and she moved up to the stage, warbling liquid sighs when there were no words, weaving connections among the three musicians, dropping almost into a tenor at times. Garcia looked at Justin, who smiled back; Jorme was too busy with the unfamiliar autar, his brow furrowed in concentration as he tried to keep up with the veteran musicians, sweat dripping down his cheeks. The woman moved over to him and mopped his face, then did the same for Justin and Garcia.

Finally they stopped and the owner brought them great mugs of beer. Garcia had never cared much for the drink but right now anything cold felt good.

"What's your name?" he asked the woman.

"A name. What does it matter?" She touched her face. "They call me Parakeet or Warbler or Thrush or Canary. It changes but the meaning's always the same. Will you play some more?"

Garcia nodded. "You will sing?" She nodded back.

More mugs of beer joined the empty ones on stage and suddenly there was money, the paper of the *barraque*, coins, thrust at them. Justin picked it up and gave it to the woman: "Take it. We don't need it." She hesitated then scooped up the money.

Garcia looked at Jorme, who was grinning dazedly. "How did you like that?"

"It was more fun than the concerts."

It was. There had been an immediacy to their playing that had never been present during a concert. The playing had been ragged and frequently out-of-tune, since neither he nor Jorme was familiar with the instruments they were playing, and the three of them had never played together before. It all had to come out from inside them — they couldn't rely on technique and ability alone. If he could just get this spirit during a performance or a recording... but it was gone, only a memory now, and it would have to be recaptured again and again. It could never be recreated or relived; each time would be different.

There was a glow of accomplishment and achievement Garcia had not felt since those few short weeks he had spent playing in the Row Jimmy after Stella Blue's death. Garcia had forgotten this feeling in the intervening years. He hoped he would never forget it again. There were a peace and a satisfaction he had not known possible. It was obvious Jorme was feeling something similar, as was the woman. Justin seemed to be less touched by the moment.

The crowd was beginning to disperse; their audience was moving away. Garcia began to play softly on the old guitar, Jorme and Justin joined, and the music began to build in intensity again...

...and the night erupted in light. Outside the dingy bar an intense white actinic light flared and grew, seeming to die in intensity as their eyes became accustomed to it, but still bright.

"What the...?" Justin's voice was drowned out in cries of *"Svana! Svana!"*

Svana! Garcia had heard the word during his short stay in the *barraque* five years earlier but he had never actually seen one of the spontaneous impromptu religious festivals. No one was interested in their music now. A *svana* parade was happening and that took precedence over anything else in the *barraque*.

He laid his instrument down on the old stand and moved toward the door, following the crowd... he who prided himself on never following the crowd.

"You ever seen one of these things before?" he asked Jorme.

"A couple."

"What is it?" Justin asked.

"*Svana*. It's some kind of religious festival."

"The celebration of rebirth," Jorme said. "The celebration of the day when all men shall be judged and the *barraquistes* will receive their true reward."

"Sounds like wish fulfillment to me," Justin said.

"Of course." Garcia smiled. "That's all that religions ever are."

Jorme looked at him with a hard light in his eyes. "Don't let any of the *barraquistes* hear you say that. A lot of them take *svana* very seriously, and they don't take kindly to criticism."

Standing on a chair outside the doorway, Garcia could see the procession coming down the street. Platforms carried on the back of *barraque* men, themselves hidden by black felt or satin that brushed the dirty bricks of the street. The platforms covered with flowers and blooms, red a favorite color, red, the color of blood. In the middle of the platforms, statues of a man—always the same man, in different poses, long hair flowing down to his waist—sometimes blond hair, sometimes black, one a rust color, one a gray. The man was naked to the waist, his face a study of agony and compassion; he seemed to be grieving for the pain of the *barraque*—the stone eyes of the statues appeared to sweep through the crowd, always focusing on the observer, following him, staring at him, judging him, until the eyes were obscured from sight and it was time to face the next statue.

On some floats the statue stood tall, its hand held out in a greeting or blessing. Still the eyes touched Garcia and continued to hold him in that compassionate yet stern gaze. On others the man was sitting with legs crossed, his head crowned with a tiara of thorns from which red roses bloomed like bursts of blood. On one, he rose on one knee, imploring.

Not all the statues were statues, however. Garcia realized that some of them were actual models, holding one pose for hours until muscles had to scream for release, then went beyond that phase to acceptance, the same acceptance of suffering that appeared in their eyes.

On either side of the street, men followed the floats, holding aloft heavy poles that carried the actinic floodlights that had first alerted the *barraquistes* of the *svana* parade's approach. The scent of incense was heavy in the air, so heavy it seemed one could not continue to breathe any longer, the air as thick as puree.

Garcia became of others pacing slowly alongside the floats, men and women in soft black hoods, black silk tunics, and woven belts. They were all barefoot; some carried the large candles from which came the incense that clung in the air.

A voice at Garcia's side cut through the incense-laden air. The girl who had been singing with them now was singing to the *svana* floats, to the martyred man whose statues now gazed down at her with compassion and understanding. Another voice, good but not as pure as hers, answered from the other side of the street and soon the *barraque* night was filled with wordless songs of aching need and desire.

Men stood in the street with tears streaming down their faces, the hard faces of *barraque* men, hard-muscled, intense weary eyes, many of them with their heads covered with handkerchiefs. Their heads were bowed, their bodies bent.

Garcia was aware not only of the girl who stood nearby, her voice once again silent, but also of Augie standing there, his slow mind moved by the spectacle which he had undoubtedly witnessed countless times, and yet did not fully understand.

Then the last of the floats was gone and their eyes had to become reaccustomed to the sudden darkness as the sounds and music receded in the distance.

"That's impressive," Garcia said. "I'd never really felt the power of superstition before."

"It's more than..." Jorme was interrupted as someone grabbed Garcia from behind and whirled him around so rapidly that he stumbled as he tried to maintain his balance.

He found himself face to face with a hawk-nosed, lean-faced *barraquiste*, his eyes hard with anger under the kerchief. "What did you say?"

"I only... I'm sorry..."

"The *svana* be more than superstition."

"I didn't mean..."

"I hear you play." The *barraquiste* gestured toward the empty bandstand. "You be good but that give you no right..."

"I didn't mean..."

A hand slammed against his face. "You listen me, you! Just 'cause you play so good, you no better than me. You no better than the mud on the streets!"

"Now wait a minute!" Jorme moved his lean body between them and another *barraquiste* tried to pull him away but the young autarist shoved him clumsily. The *barraquiste* fell against the brick building, his head making a sickening crunch against the stone. For a moment there was a sphere of silence around them, then there was a grunt of inarticulate rage from the *barraquistes,* and Jorme disappeared under a mass of bodies.

Augie began pulling the men away. There was the sound of sirens. The *barraquistes* melted into the night, taking with them the body of their comrade.

Garcia knelt beside Jorme, all the joy and happiness of the evening gone. Blood welled out from a dozen cuts, but the worst seemed to be two stomach wounds. "Garcia? Tell Pentland... tell her..."

"Yes?"

"I loved her. I really did."

"You'll be all right, Jorme. Damn it. You've got to be all right. Hold on; the police are on their way."

"I've called an ambulance," the owner of the bar said from the entrance.

"You hear that, Jorme? Just hold on."

But Jorme just arched his body in a spasm that had to be painful beyond bearing, and let out a groan that expressed far less than the pain he had to be experiencing.

Chapter 27

"It looks like we're going to have a busy night," the attendant said as the ambulance flew toward the hospital.

"How's that?" Justin asked as Garcia stared glumly at Jorme's still form. The attendants already had him connected to machines, but the signs were bad.

"The *'quistes* are rioting again. We always have some rough-and-tumbles whenever they have one of these festivals. But it looks like it's going to be worse tonight." Neither Justin nor Garcia said anything but he continued anyway. "Someone said something about immortality."

"Immortality?" Garcia looked up sharply at the attendant.

"Yeah. Can you beat that? They're saying they want to be immortal, and they're going to tear the city down until they are. You ever heard anything so crazy? If that's what religion does to you, I don't want none of it."

Garcia looked back at Jorme. "Is he all right? I thought I saw a needle waver."

"Maybe. Those instruments are pretty sensitive. Can't really tell nothing till we get him back to the hospital. I think he'll pull through. Those wounds look pretty superficial. Probably not deep enough to do any real damage."

Garcia didn't know whether or not to believe the attendant. He spoke the words like a well-memorized litany, without any depth or feeling, as though he'd said them to hundreds of people on hundreds of similar occasions.

When they reached the hospital, Jorme was whisked away, still unconscious, while Justin and Garcia were led to an office, where a clerk took down details and information. When they were done, forms spit out from the machine at his desk. Justin and Garcia scanned them quickly and put their prints at the bottom.

"How is Jorme?" Garcia asked impatiently.

"Just a minute." The clerk was silent, communing with the hospital's computer. "He is fine. He is resting well."

"He'll recover?"

"We will contact you as soon as there is a change in his condition." Garcia slumped back against the wall, dissatisfied with the clerk's answer, but knowing it would be futile to try to get more out of him. Had Bwire felt this way when Garcia had disappeared into the *barraque*, worrying over the fate of his protégé, damning himself for the part he had played in bringing it about?

The door opened and a policeman walked in. "Mr. Garcia? Mr. Mead? I'm here to escort you home."

"I'm staying here," Garcia said, "until I know what happens to Jorme."

"I don't think that would be wise, sir. There's a riot in the *barraque* and it may well threaten the rest of the city. The hospital will be quite busy. You'll only be in the way." Garcia recognized the tone: they did not want him here and he would be removed, by force if necessary.

"We will let you know if there is any improvement," the clerk said as they left.

꙾ ❮ ❯ ꙾

The streets of the city were empty and deserted; only an occasional police car passed them, going in the opposite direction. Once Garcia thought he saw a tank moving on a parallel street but it was too brief a glimpse to be sure.

"It wasn't your fault," Justin said when they reached his apartment building. "There was nothing you could've done."

"Sure, Justin."

"I'd come up with you but I have to get home to my wife. I hate the thought of you being alone up there right now. Why don't you come home with me tonight?"

"No, thanks. I've got to call Pentland."

"You could call her from my place."

"Thanks, Justin, but I'd rather be here."

As he rode the elevator to his apartment, he thought about it: *No, it wasn't his fault. Not his fault at all. Who had suggested they go out for a night on the town? Who had begun the fight by slighting the* barraquiste's *religion?* No matter what Justin said or thought, Garcia had to take the responsibility. His actions had led inexorably to Jorme's injuries, and possible death. He was responsible; he could not ignore it or refuse it.

The thought of calling Pentland and telling her what had happened left a cold lump in Garcia's stomach. He dreaded the call, but it had to be made, and he was the one who had to make it.

As soon as he entered the apartment, however, the supervisor notified him that Shaara had been trying all evening to get in touch with him. "Shall I place a return call?" it asked.

"Not yet. Get me in touch with Pentland LaCroix first."

He sank down wearily in one of the apartment's more comfortable chairs, its form adjusting itself to his body. "Get me a drink." The supervisor began preparing a green joe.

"Garcia?" Pentland's form materialized on the holostage. "Is Jorme there? I've been trying to get him all night."

"He's in the hospital, Pentland."

"No! What happened?"

Briefly, Garcia told her what had happened, making no attempt to play down his own role in his protégé's injuries. She seemed to stiffen as he talked to her about it.

"You don't know...?"

"They said they'd let me know if there was any change."

"I'm going down there."

"Good luck. They kicked *me* out. Let me know as soon as there's any change, will you?"

Pentland paused a moment, her eyes hard and cold. "All right. I will. Goodbye, Garcia."

"Good luck. I hope everything turns out."

He took a long drink from his green joe as Pentland's form faded away. "Do you wish me to contact Shaara now?" his supervisor asked.

"No. Not yet." His head was spinning, still trying to digest the night's events. It seemed no matter what he did, it was wrong. It had been his own desire for excitement and companionship that had driven him out into the night, taking Jorme and Justin with him, willy-nilly, down to the *barraque*. He should have known better. Shaara would never have done anything so silly. Did he have some kind of death wish? But hadn't Shaara's own life become a kind of death in itself?

He looked around the room, where he had once been the court balladeer, the minstrel, where it seemed he had played the fool instead. He felt like a worm climbing up a rose plant, trying to get past the thorns to the beautiful... and edible... bloom above. And when he reached one flower, it faded in his grasp and he saw one further up still more beautiful. To get to it he had to struggle through the thorns, the threatened impalement. But without the thorns, there would be no rose, and the worm would wither and die.

"Shaara would like to talk to you."

Startled by the supervisor's voice, he gripped the glass he had been holding even harder and it shattered, stabbing a painful thorn of plastic into his wrist.

"Let me talk to her."

Shaara materialized on the holostage, facing the chair where Garcia normally sat, but he was behind her, by the bookcase and its emergency exit, nursing the minor wound to his wrist.

"Garcia." She turned around, looking for him. "Oh, there you are. Where have you...? Darling, have you hurt yourself?"

"Just a little." The blood was a bright red, the vibrant color of life.

She peered at him. "Are you sure?" Her look of concern became one almost of scorn. "I don't know what to do about you. Sometimes you act just like a child."

"Is that what you wanted to talk to me about?"

"No, of course not. I've been trying to get you all night. Where have you *been*?"

"I know. I..."

"There are riots going on. They say they're going to be worse than the food riots. There are people outside my father's estate right now."

"Shaara, listen..."

"We're all going out to father's country estate, where we'll be safe. I'll have father send a police flyer over to pick you up and you can join us there."

"Shaara, I'm not going."

"I've been so worried about you, Garcia. How could you do something like this at such a time?"

"Shaara, I'm not going."

"Don't be silly, Garcia. It's not safe here. Of course, this will delay your final operation a bit, but at least you'll be safe."

"I'm not taking the operation, Shaara."

"What are you talking about? Of course you are."

Garcia told her what had happened that night. Her terrified face grew even more frightened.

"What's the matter with you, darling? You could have been killed."

"What about poor Jorme? He may die yet."

"Of course. But it's you I worry about. This only makes it clearer: You've got to come out and join us, stay with me permanently. Now. Surely you can see that."

"I can see that I'm not going to take that final operation. I'm going to stay here with Jorme and Justin and Pentland and the people I belong with."

"You belong with me, darling. Don't you want to be immortal?"

"Yes, of course. But..." How could he explain it to her? How could he make her understand? She didn't see the life she was living as a kind of death, but to him... "Don't you see, Shaara? Without the worm, there would be no rose."

"What are you talking about?"

"Never mind. I'm staying here, Shaara. I'm not going to take your damned operation."

"You know what this means, don't you, Garcia? I can't marry you, if you're not one of us."

"I understand."

"But I love you, Garcia. I really do. I'll always remember you."

"I love you too, Shaara. But I can't live your way."

"Goodbye, my love."

They stood there, each facing the other's intangible image for a long moment, then Shaara broke the connection.

I'll always remember you. He wondered if she really would. Always would probably be a very long time for Shaara.

He began pacing the apartment but nothing held his attention for very long. He went into the workroom and stared out at the city for a long moment. There seemed to be no difference. The riot was big, but could not yet be seen on this panorama. He took out the old autar, and the old guitar, and played each of them briefly, but he could not finish even one melody.

Something in him called out for action, to do something more than just play an instrument. He recalled that moment of exaltation back in the *barraque* bar, when the restlessness that had dogged him for so many months was silent and pacified. Now it was back, stronger than ever. He realized it would always come back, leaving whenever he started something new, returning when it was time to move onward. Only if he were immortal would it be gone forever.

He returned to the main room, with its false bookcases and its false fireplace. He remembered when Jorme had first come to him, with his awkward hands and his nervous manner. He remembered the strength and beauty of Jorme's concerts, and he remembered the night that he and Pentland had stood on the edge of the roof while Garcia had cowered near the elevator housing.

Bwire's last message to Garcia was on a table next to the fireplace: *There is something growing inside you, a restlessness. I don't know its exact cause but please don't disregard it. Follow it, Garcia. It may be hard at times but you will not regret it. Reach, strive. Go over the edge.*

Garcia opened the emergency exit and started up the barren stairway to the roof. Once again he stood in the doorway of the housing, his heart pounding, looking out into the windy night. Now, with the panorama of the entire city spread out on all sides, he could see groups of lights he hadn't noticed from his apartment. Down by the river, a glow flickered, and further on there was another fire.

He walked out from the elevator housing, trembling, and the wind hit him full force, threatening to tear him away from the roof into the night. It carried with it the faint smell of smoke, of burning timbers. It paused, as if to gather strength, and in the silence Garcia could hear the sounds of sirens and of distant amplified voices, the faint echo of shouts of rage, of tiny cheers.

He looked down over the dizzying edge of the building, where a flimsy rail was all that prevented him from a stomach-wrenching plunge down countless stories. If his heart was pounding now, it was not in fear but in exultation. He was *alive*, come what may, come death and extinction, as surely it must. You can't go back, he thought, and you can't stand still. He had to go forward or he would surely die. That was where his strength, and his art lay, in the constant fight against Death, spitting in its very face, not in conquering it and then living in a fearful immortality. So he would die. So what? In the meantime, he would live life to its fullest, not cringing before every tiny germ.

He started back from the edge of the roof, his mind aglow like the fires in the *barraque*. Bwire's unfinished compositions waited for him, but the melody of another composition was forming in his mind. It would start out in a sad, plaintive key—D minor perhaps—but it would end in a triumphant, surging G major. It would be for autar, guitar, and flute, and there would be a part in it for the beautiful soaring voice of a girl with a scarred face.

He stopped in the doorway of the elevator housing and looked back at the city, watching the flickering glow of the fires and smelling their smoke in the wind.

He would call his composition simply *The Edge*.

Shaara would never understand.

ON THE DECK OF THE STARSHIP

The starship orbited Earth. It was being constructed around the shell of an asteroid whose orbit had neared that of Earth, and which been captured by a team of astronauts. It had been building for ten years, an ungodly collection of pods and experimental sections that would carry seven thousand gypsies past the sun, beyond Pluto, beyond the comet-spawning zone that marked the borders of the solar system, gathering speed as it gulped hydrogen atoms, sailing toward light-speed. It would take two years to get past Pluto's orbit, most of its crew in cryogenic sleep, reaching out in an attempt to lengthen the lifetime of humanity beyond that of its own solar system, a feeble attempt at immortality for Mankind.

Less than one percent of the population had volunteered for its crew and passenger list but it had taken several years for the computers to sift through that small percentage of Mankind's billions, trying to reach a balance between races, skills, intelligence, physical abilities, education, and a myriad of other criteria.

Even so, some people had to be actively recruited, people whose talents were rare and needed.

Primrose Young was not one of those. She had been in love with the project from its inception, when she was still halfway through grammar school, a little flower of a ten-year-old girl. She had grown up with one thought in mind: she was going to be on the crew of the starship. She had studied all the disciplines she thought would be needed: chemistry, cybernetics, astronautics, nuclear physics, computer science. She was certain her talents would cause her to be chosen for the crew.

But she was only one of tens of thousands who had the same idea and dream, who had grown up pointing themselves arrow-like at the starship. Only a mere handful, slightly less than a hundred of those tens of thousands would be chosen.

Philip Steinbrunner couldn't have cared less. He knew about the starship, of course, but it was of no importance to him. His world was the theatre: it was his universe, and he had no need to go out into the galaxy. Nightly, behind his bottle-thick eyeglasses, he orchestrated the live performances of the city theatre, his stubby fingers passing glibly over the keys of the computer terminal. The electrical impulses so generated became multiplied a thousandfold inside the computer, channeled and redirected, flowing to lights and machines, slowly bringing set pieces in and out, fading lights slowly or bringing on instant black-outs, creating sunsets complete with robin songs. If he could have controlled the actors, he would have done that too, and with consummate precision, perhaps even art. But Philip did not consider himself an artist: he was merely a craftsman, a technician. Those in the trade knew of his skills and ability; the actors knew he was good, but they dismissed him since he was not an actor; the public assumed that the success and brilliance of the theatre were completely the responsibility of the director and the actors. Philip Steinbrunner knew all this and he didn't care. All that mattered to him was the creation of precision and the exponential performance curve that would never quite bring him to perfection.

Where Philip Steinbrunner was thick fingers, pear-shaped body, a fringe of scanty, reddish-blond whiskers, with a deceptive clumsiness, Primrose Young was all curves and grace. She was a lithe, dainty girl with delicate breasts, and gentle, well-curved legs. Her face was squarish, firm, and dedicated; it should not have gone well with that delicate body, but somehow it worked. She was not pretty or beautiful, but she attracted plenty of men. She would have looked even better if her dark hair had been long and flowing, but she kept it cropped short, almost mannish, to keep it out of the way of her experiments. For Primrose Young was just as adept in the laboratory as Philip Steinbrunner was in the theatre. Her tapered fingers flew across laboratory consoles in a dance that was as graceful as Philip's was earthbound. She could find reagents and crucibles and solve four-body problems and Korbyshev polynomials as easily as he faded lights and rearranged sets.

They should never have known each other. By all the rules that govern such things, they should never have even met. He was Caliban to her Miranda. Their worlds were Venn diagrams that should not have intersected, but they had one point in common. The name of that point was Linda Fortino. She was a casual friend of Primrose's and a friend of a friend of Philip's. Somehow they both got invited to the same party at Linda's.

As usual, Primrose was one of the first to arrive at the party. Linda Fortino's current lover, an engineering student, had just assembled his own light organ, and he delighted in showing the instrument off. He let other people try to create their own light shows with it, but no one came close to doing as well as Primrose. Not even Linda's lover himself could do as well as Primrose.

After several people had played with the instrument, she sat down at the console and began hitting keys at random, learning what effects they would cause, finding the blue lights, the green lights, the strobes, the amoebas, the slides, the flashers. She learned to regulate the timings, to slow down and speed up, and when she was finished, she accepted the congratulations with aplomb and casual amusement. After all, she knew she was as good with a computer as they come, better than anyone else she knew.

So when Philip shambled in and was urged to try out the light show, she smiled to herself. This clumsy male in the ill-fitting clothes could not even do as well as most of the others. She wondered why they urged him to try it and she felt a moment of pity for him and once again thanked her stars that she was so talented and lucky.

She was a little surprised when he obtained simple but tasteful patterns by his slow tentative approach to the computer. Despite his clumsiness and shyness and awkwardness with people, he seemed to have a flare for creation.

"Not bad," she remarked condescendingly to no one in particular.

"Wait," someone close to her said.

She turned around in irritation but couldn't figure out who had said it.

Already the show was gaining in complexity, gathering momentum for a fireworks display of green carnations and violet nebulae. It was not the cold, cool, calculated precision light-play of the competent computer-player. There was such an element present, but there was more. A dark gray of depressions shaded rapidly through purples and reds into a brilliant orange crescendo of happiness that ran over the walls. The orange chased the gray around the room and devoured it, even as the orange itself was being devoured by the cool green of contemplation, which disintegrated in a shower of bright blue and yellow streamers, culminating in protons and falling stars, gamma rays, and starships, streaking fleshtones, rich brown planets, orbiting white stars, mountains and Irish whiskeys, prophets on the mountains and feather headbands. With a final burst of color, Philip settled down to a leaf storm that danced in autumns around the room, quiet and gentle.

There would have been applause had anyone known he was finished, but Philip was in his element. Having explored the machine and pushed it to its limits (which were far beyond those its creator had thought possible), he now worked gently and unobtrusively with the music. People drifted off, to dance, drink, talk, make love, or just watch his patterns.

Primrose, now utterly crushed, knowing Philip had surpassed her smug, but sterile, production as easily as she had surpassed the others at the party, watched him as he played at the light organ, totally immersed, and absorbed.

"Care for a sniff?" someone asked her.

She shook her head, turned away, and went looking for Linda Fortino. When she found her hostess, she asked, "Who is that weird-looking guy at the computer? He's good."

"Oh, he's a friend of Jerry's. Has something to do with the theatre. Jerry's a dancer, you know. He's really playing up a storm, isn't he?"

Primrose nodded. She didn't know who Jerry was, and she didn't much care. She walked back to the light organ and stood behind Philip, watching as his clumsy blunt fingers moved skillfully over the keyboard. It was hard to believe that such awkward, and apparently random, movement could produce such beauty.

Philip looked up at her and smiled briefly. She smiled back, but he was already re-absorbed in his show. Half a minute later, aware she was still watching him, he recorded a simple twenty-five-minute instruction loop, put the organ on automatic, and turned back to Primrose.

"You like it?" he asked, smiling like a child.

"It's very good. Could you teach me to do that?"

He frowned. "I don't know. I'm not very good at teaching people things."

She sat down next to him. "Just try."

From there, things progressed as such things progress, in great leaps, and in clumsy bounds, looping back upon themselves and getting caught in the capstans. Primrose got Philip to agree to let her come over to the theatre, where he showed off his skill at setting up scenes and changing lights. He let her run the computer, more complicated in its way than those of the laboratory. Whereas she was used to the delicacy of control necessary in the laboratory, she was not accustomed to the complexity of operations, the number of degrees of movement and ability necessary for the theatre. Philip watched over her like a mother hen, ready to pounce if she should put his precious equipment in danger.

She stood behind him while he ran an actual production, and she watched as the actors and actresses left with barely a word for him.

"They don't even know you exist," she said. "They take you for granted."

"I'm just part of the machinery." He grinned as though that was the most natural thing in the world.

"But that's not right. If it wasn't for you, they couldn't do anything."

"It's unimportant." He reached up to switch off the computer. The faint electrical sound that had become a part of them all for several hours died with a barely perceptible whimper. "You appreciate what I'm doing, and I know when I've done a good job. What do they matter? They're just actors." It was a long speech for Philip and he grinned in embarrassment.

That was the first night Primrose slept with him. The first of many. Philip didn't live for others' approbation; he lived to satisfy only himself, and yet he did so without imposing his will or presence on others. As long as they left him alone to do what he wanted to do, he was happy. It was a refreshing change from the tense competitiveness with which Primrose had grown up.

They walked into the electric park together one night when the theatre was dark. Philip hadn't wanted to; he wanted to go back to the theatre and explore the computer still more. There was a scene in the current production he wasn't satisfied with. He felt a slight change in one of the sets could result in a smoother transition.

"Not tonight, Philip," she said. "It can wait, can't it?"

"Sure. But there's nothing more important that needs to be done, so why not do it now?"

"Can't we spend tonight together alone for once?"

"We'll be alone in the theatre."

But Philip had little experience withstanding someone else's desires, so he went with her. She found a section that was dark, checked the time, and pointed to the sky. "Look up, Philip, you'll be able to see it pretty soon."

They watched in silence for a few moments then the ship appeared magically in the sky. Hidden in Earth's shadow, it hadn't caught sunlight until it was almost at the zenith. Now it moved rapidly across the sky, twinkling and fading as its rotation reflected sunlight from different facets.

"What do you think?" she asked when it was gone.

"It was nice," Philip said.

"Nice? Is that all you can say about it? It's the hope of mankind."

"Well, I was just thinking..." Philip's voice trailed off, but Primrose said nothing. She had become accustomed to his thoughtful pauses by now and knew better than to interrupt his train of thinking. "If we moved a couple of those stars, and maybe put a little more color in the twinkling of the starship..."

"*Moved* the stars?" Primrose asked incredulously.

"Yeah," Philip said eagerly. "You know, and maybe a little more wind in the trees." He clapped his hands together. "Don't you think that would be more effective?"

"Philip, Philip," she said, like a mother to a little child. "This is reality. We can't do things like that."

Philip looked thoughtfully up at the sky, his chin cupped in one hand. "Yeah," he said at last, "but I can do it in the theatre."

ം‹›ം

She took him to the laboratory with her one day and let him play with her computer, watching him as he had watched her in the theatre, but he made no mistakes. He did exactly what she told him to do, following the instructions she called up from the computer's memory banks. By the time the afternoon had come to its end, he was carrying on three experiments at a time, moving deftly from one console to another. She intervened only when two experiments reached critical phases at the same time.

"That was poor timing," he said later. "If I'd known that was going to happen, I'd have started one of them sooner."

"Philip," she said, laughing, "you're incorrigible."

"I try to be," he said.

"You ought to apply for the starship. You're a natural."

"Why should I do that? They don't have a theatre up there."

"But, Philip... you can do just about anything you want with a computer. I've never seen anything like it. You don't even understand half the things you're doing, I'm sure of it, but you... you're like part of the computer."

Philip smiled proudly. "We're a team."

In the small apartment they now shared, he watched as she went through her exercises, toning up for the semi-weightless conditions of the starship. He stayed out of her way, all too well aware of his own clumsiness away from his beloved computers.

"You ought to do them, too," she said. "They'd be good for you."

"I'm in good shape," he replied.

"Besides, if you changed your mind, you'd be all set for the starship. You'd have a lot less work to do."

"I'm not applying for it," he said, quietly, matter-of-factly.

Primrose Young had not been the first woman to pay attention to Philip. Starstruck struggling actresses had tried to use him as a stepping-stone, tying themselves to his coat strings as a way into the world of successful theatre. Some had even succeeded in establishing careers as bit actresses. Philip had simply given a mental shrug or two, and accepted their attention when he had it, missing it only briefly when it was gone.

But Primrose was something else. She wasn't using him as a stepping-stone for her own career. She had her own brilliant career going, one that had nothing to do with Philip Steinbrunner's world. He had accepted her placidly at first, soon learning of her obsession with the starship. It was just another part of her, unimportant at the time, since Philip thought she would just pass through his life as so many other people had.

But it didn't turn out that way this time. They grew together in a way he had never known before and, when she was accepted for the starship crew, he was unprepared.

"What'll I do?" Primrose asked, caught between her love for Philip and the need to satisfy her obsession. There were tears in her eyes but she wasn't yet crying.

"You'll do what you have to do," he said calmly, but beneath the calmness, a frantic part of his soul was begging to be set loose.

"I can't leave you," she said. "You've got to come with me."

"They won't let me," he said reasonably, shutting the door firmly on his screaming soul. "I don't have any skills they need. What place would a theatre technician have on a new world?"

"You could come as my mate, my husband. They'd have to let you come."

Philip smiled sadly. Only the echoes of his screaming soul were left. "No, they wouldn't, and you know it. They'd just replace you." The back of his hand brushed a snifter and Primrose caught it before it tumbled to the floor. "And what makes you think I'd want to go?"

"You wouldn't go?" Primrose looked at him in astonishment. She had never really considered the fact that anyone might not want to go on the starship.

"Of course not. I have everything I need right here. On the starship, I'd have nothing to do."

"But I can't stay here," she cried. "I have to go."

"Of course you do. I understand." He quickly cut off a faint wail from his soul. "You won't be happy if you don't go, and I won't be happy if I do."

"You don't love me," she accused.

"Of course I do."

Then the weeks ran like water over marble; there was little time now to share the electric dawns as they had once done. Their moments together were brief and passionate until finally Primrose was gone from Philip's life, orbiting over his head in the year's training and acclimatization she would undergo before the starship finally departed.

And Philip Steinbrunner could ignore his soul no longer.

Everything began to look like scenery stored in an empty theatre, stars on the ground, fences in the sky, and rips and tears in the curtain of time. On his free nights, he went to the electric park to watch the twinkling starship streak overhead. Somewhere in that ungainly jumble, Primrose was preparing to leave Earth, and Philip Steinbrunner, behind.

It wasn't that he missed their infrequent lovemaking: their passion had primarily been one of minds, and she had pointed out doors to him he had never bothered to notice before.

At last, Philip went to the agency in charge of recruiting and training starship crew members.

"I'm sorry," the administrator said after Philip had filled out a plethora of forms and taken scores of tests. "I'm afraid there is no place for you in the starship program, Mr. Steinbrunner. We're all very much impressed with your talents, especially your ability with computers, but there are just too many holes in your scientific background."

Undaunted, Philip turned inquisitor, drawing from the administrator the disciplines in which they were most interested.

"You're wasting your time, Mr. Steinbrunner," the administrator said. "There's no possible way you could become proficient enough in these fields in time to make the starship crew."

ᔦᐊᐅᔧ

He attacked the problem with an obsession that would have astounded Primrose Young, and that did astound the people in the theatre world who were used to an easy-going Philip Steinbrunner. He severed all his ties with the theatre, then dove deeply into the computer, spending twelve to sixteen hours a day at it, learning about approach spirals, ecological degradation, quasars, positions, organ transplantation, learning cyborg technology, and a dozen other things he had not known existed. He mastered set theory in three days; trigonometry took a little longer. Calculus eluded him until the theory of the point of accumulation, when all the threads came together in one glorious conclusion. Two hours later, he was once again confused. Relativity, quantum physics, organic chemistry, all were mastered to the point where Philip knew just how to query the computer on those points he had forgotten, or had never known in the first place.

Philip became a true renaissance man in an age of specialists, not knowing perhaps as deeply and intuitively as a specialist, but aware of the nebulous bridges between disciplines. The combination of knowledge in two or more different areas sometimes brought him to conclusions no one else had yet arrived at. His understanding of computers, their abilities, and their shortcomings, fused with his new knowledge of organ transplantation and cyborg technology to convince him those transplants considered "impossible" were indeed not so: any transplant was possible for an experienced surgeon teamed with a computer operator of Philip's ability controlling the supportive functions.

The technicians at the agency were amazed.

"It's impossible," they told the administrator. "The guy's absolutely incredible. There's only one other person on the starship who even approaches him."

"But it's too late," the administrator said. "The starship leaves in two months. The crew and backups all been chosen, trained and acclimated. There isn't enough time or room for another man and his support equipment and supplies."

"Never mind," said Philip. "Let me finish the course. Perhaps you'll need me after all. Perhaps there'll be a delay. Perhaps there'll be another starship."

"There'll be no other starship, and there'll be no major delays," the administrator said. "And we will not needing you. You should have started this years ago. There's no way you can make the starship now."

"Yes, there is," Philip said softly.

He looked down at himself through the video pickups of the operating room. He was connected directly to a computer through electrodes implanted into his brain. He couldn't feel them or sense them; the brain has no sensory input of its own. He would be guiding his own surgery, through computer-controlled waldos, aided by the computer's massive memory. He knew more than any surgeon, had exquisite control, and microsecond precision. He no longer needed those blunt, stubby, clumsy-looking fingers. His fingers now were made of steel and aluminum and ended in saws and pincers and whatever other tools he needed.

Philip Steinbrunner was in his element now. He no longer was part of the computer, nor was the computer an extension of his body and wishes; he and the computer were one.

Primrose Young floated gently to the aleph "floor" of the computer room. Her scalp had been shaved; lesions showed where dozens of pinpoint receptacles waited for their mates in the computer helmet that slipped easily over her head. There were none of the clumsy, inefficient, slow keyboard consoles for the starship's computer banks.

Primrose strapped herself into the chair and settled the helmet over her head, feeling the insertion of the electrodes in an almost sexual manner. This was not by chance; the designers of the system had included several psychologists.

With her head now hooked into the Andromeda computer, she said "Ready" into the mouthpiece.

A new component had arrived less than twenty-four hours earlier and was being mated to the system. There was quite a lot of attention being devoted to it.

A red light blinked on in Primrose's head, turning immediately to green. She thought the anagram that opened the circuits. One by one, she entered the gates of the computer, feeling its resistance to her entry fall rapidly to zero. At each stage, she and the computer were tested to make sure that both were ready and compatible. At last she stood before the new module. There was a longer delay here before contact was completed.

"Hello?" The voice that resonated in her mind was the mechanical computer-voice she always created in her brain but it was yet somehow familiar. Something in the pauses, the way words were emphasized, banged at the doors of her subconscious.

"This is computer technician Primrose Young," she replied, "activating test sequence 48-Gauss-polynomial-three. The constants for this test are..."

"Relax, Primrose," the voice said. "We don't have to go through all that."

Her subconscious finished its connections and Philip's voice replaced the mechanical monotone.

"But... where are you?" she asked. "The new module..."

"...is too small for a complete human being," he finished for her. "No, there wasn't enough time left to acclimatize my body for the starship. But they needed my brain almost as much as I need to be with you."

For a moment she failed to understand, then the true impact and horror of what he had done reached her. "Oh, Philip," was all she could say.

He caught the pity and dismay in her tone and replied, "Don't be sorry for me, Primrose. It's what I wanted. Really."

"Oh, but, Philip..."

"Remember what Shakespeare said."

"Shakespeare?"

"'All the world's a stage.'"

"Yes."

"He was thinking small. I have the whole universe as my theatre now.

↘◄►↙

Slowly the starship moved out of its orbit, leaving Earth's gravity cage, toward Mars, then beyond, past Uranus and Pluto, breaking through, moving on out to the cold and the dark.

If you've only lived on Earth, you've never really seen the sun or known the promise of the village of stars. You can't move the stars. But you can move yourself, and that can make just as much difference. Ask Philip Steinbrunner. He feels the planets in his body and he regrets nothing.

THE WORM BENEATH THE SKULL

The smell of rotting sea creatures mixed with that of rotting fruit in the hot dry air of the city of Brokedown Palace on Clayton's Peacock, a minor planet out near the rim. Newshawks shoved newscopies in my face and a beggar clutched my ankle. "A nixie for Allah, lady?" he asked tremulously but I pulled myself free.

I pushed my way through the crowded market section of the *barraque*, curious to find out what was causing the noise I had been hearing for several minutes. It sounded like someone was torturing some poor animal, but no one else seemed to be bothered by the noise – they wandered slowly and aimlessly, searching for bargains, while I cursed them silently as I fought my way through.

I'd never before heard such painful sounds carried to such interminable lengths, yet I kept thinking I could somehow use it in a song. People are always interested in the pain of others.

I turned the corner of a crumbling building and came out on a small plaza, where a small group of tourists and *barraquistes* surrounded an old beggar playing a violin in a keyhole archway on the other side of the plaza. Behind him, the sprinkled scant stars of the outer rim faded down to the greenish glow of the horizon. No one in his audience seemed upset by the raucous sawing of his violin. Or by his appearance.

His face was white and smooth, as hard and as calcified as bone, his hair a pure white frazzle that stuck out in all directions. His nasal cavity was just a hole in the skullface, and the drawn-back lips had become a skull's grin. The pair of blood-red electroglasses that covered his eye-sockets matched the color of his robe.

The hands that emerged from the carmine robe were thin and skeletal, and ended in viciously sharp claws. Two bracelets dangled limply from one bone-thin wrist.

As I moved closer, the music seemed to alter. There was a pattern to his playing but it took me a while to recognize the tune as Wainer's Cepheian rondo. To tell the truth, he was doing a rather credible job on the music, but the scraping of those bony fingers on the strings of the instrument, and the uncontrolled waver of the notes, were almost unbearable.

The music seemed to hesitate momentarily, stumbling, then it picked up, even stronger than before. It was eerie and strangely compelling, evoking memories of passion, with images of violent death swirling through mad unbridled joy, tempered with grief – a bacchanal of conflicting emotions – ending on a black and despairing note I somehow knew was the end, even though it hung incomplete in the air.

The violinist picked up a battered cup and passed it into the small crowd. For a moment those crimson electroglasses focused on me, and I felt an uncontrollable shiver go through me. I turned and left, fleeing almost, eager to get away from this skeletal pied piper.

I went back to my room and toyed with my autar for a few minutes. It was futile: I couldn't get that violinist out of my thoughts or the rapt looks on the faces of his audience, looks that had never been on the faces of any of *my* audiences. Everything about him reeked of death – the music he played, the images and emotions the music evoked, his very appearance. He was an abomination in a universe where immortality was available for the asking to anyone who was willing to put themselves into interminable debt.

I hadn't taken The Treatment yet, because I dreaded the thought of being in debt, but I would have to take it soon. I had just passed my thirtieth standard year, and the tiny indications of increasing age were beginning to make their appearance. Maybe they weren't noticeable to anyone else;

maybe, in fact, they were just products of my imagination – but it wouldn't be long before they *were* real and noticeable. I had to take The Treatment soon, even if it meant I would be in debt forever. But at least I'd be young forever as well.

I wished again for the ten-thousandth time that I had a Talent. If I was a Seer, I could be telling the leader of The Union what the future of his choices were; if I was an Empath, I could be detecting possible assassins in the crowds; if I was a Projector, I could be calming those possible assassins and others. Talents had a plush, easy life, but it came with a price: their freedom, the one thing I valued almost as much as life itself. So maybe it was just as well that I wasn't a Talent.

Sometimes I wondered what good immortality would be if I was doomed to an eternity of playing minor clubs of the rim, just one more minstrel in a universe jam-packed with minstrels. At those times I almost understood Garcia and Wainer, just two of the many who had refused The Treatment. But they had at least been recognized as artists in their own lifetimes, and had The Treatment offered them free, in fact had been begged to take it. But they had refused.

"Without the worm, there would be no rose," Garcia, the first modern master of the autar, had said. And Wainer, whose Tenth Symphony was my favorite, had walked out onto the surface of an alien planet, opened his helmet, breathed in its poisonous atmosphere, and died with a smile on his face. I mean, it's crazy enough to refuse The Treatment when you can have it free but then to go and do something like that. Don't ask me to explain it: I can't. I've never understood Wainer, and I've never understood Garcia. But, damn, the two of them wrote and played such beautiful music!

If I could do just half of what they had been capable of doing, I'd have it knocked. People would be running to hear me and I'd be able to afford The Treatment. Maybe they'd even offer it to me free. It's just not fair: those who can afford it sometimes get it free while those like me, who want it desperately but can't afford it, have to go into eternal debt. That may be okay for the groundlings, and the nine-fivers, but it's not for me.

So I was still scrounging around the rim planets, looking for something, anything, that I could turn into the song that would bring me some attention, and catapult me far from the dreary club routine to the concert circuit.

But I didn't have even the glimmer of a new song when I went to the Offnote to perform that night. The Offnote was one of the "atmosphere" clubs at the edge of the *barraque*, full of phony squalor. With a shoehorn you could get maybe a hundred and twenty people in there. The ceiling was low, and smoke from the candles on the tables hung in the air, just above the heads of the audience.

When I got there, Oaks Fahey, a local performer who was the opening act, was already on the small stage at one end of the roughly rectangular room. I stopped a waitress to order a purple joe, then went to the "back room." There were no dressing rooms at the Offnote, just the "back room" or "performers' room," where performers could dress and tune, maybe even practice a little before they went on.

I took my autar out of its case, powered up, and hit the tuning switch. The clear light lit up immediately so I powered down. Suddenly, I was feeling good. I didn't know why but I knew it had something to do with the violinist. I would go back there tomorrow and see if he was still there.

I looked at myself in the full-length holomirror. I couldn't help grinning at my image. My gray-green eyes seemed greener than ever, glinting like emeralds. I turned my face from side to side, admiring my jawline, the shape of my nose, the sheen of my red hair. I turned away from the mirror just in time to avoid the embarrassment of having the waitress come in and see me preening like that.

I took a long drink from the purple joe she gave me. It went down my throat smoothly, warming me from mouth to stomach, making me feel even better. I went out to the club and sat down at a corner table, waiting for the end of Oaks Fahey's set. Fifteen minutes after he finished, the proprietor signaled to me, and I went back to get my autar.

A couple of years ago, I went to a Ski Barnstable concert. He just walked out on stage without an introduction of any kind. Nothing. Not a word. He just walked out and started playing. Now that's class. A man who needed no introduction, so he didn't bother with one.

That's where I'd like to be some day. I'd like to pull that trick myself. But it wasn't going to happen tonight. The spotlight picked me up as I walked to the stage and the proprietor introduced me over the club's sound system: "Our featured performer, Sanchez Madeira!" As I sat down, the stage lights came up, primarily in blue. Usually I open with a moderately difficult classical piece by Wainer, just autar, no voice, but I was feeling impish this night so I began instead with "The Ballad of Stella Blue." It's a hoary old chestnut, one of the first songs I'd ever learned, and I hadn't performed it in years.

I began it *a capella*, keying in a simple rhythm as the second verse began. The rhythm, slow and basic, underlined the lyrics and set the mood for a more complex accompaniment as the song continued. By the time I was finished, I could see tears in a few eyes, and the applause was genuine and protracted, instead of the perfunctory applause I normally get.

And, of course, once you've got an audience with you, you just drive each other higher and higher.

I played a modern classical piece next, with clashing harmonies and percussive effects from the instrument's computer, a 13/16 rhythm that I bobbled several times but managed to pick up so quickly no one noticed.

I was really getting adventurous now, living close to the edge of my abilities. I did "To Morrow, Who Never Knows," an old street-song I'd learned on Mississippi Half-Step. It was a tough piece, another one I hadn't done in quite some time. I was ragged and uneven, but I managed to carry it off on sheer exuberance alone. Then I did a *mazingza*, a popular song form on Clayton's Peacock, that Oaks Fahey had taught me. Ordinarily it would be death to play a planetsong on its own homeground, but the audience loved it and I got a standing ovation and, believe me, that doesn't happen very often to Sanchez Madeira. I was dripping wet when I finally left the stage, mostly from sweat, but there were a few of my own tears mixed in there as well.

My second set wasn't nearly as good, of course, but it was a damn good one. The excitement had died down, and the set was more subdued, but I was still glowing warmly. It was a quite credible set.

The violinist was at the same spot the next day, the same keyhole archway on the same square, which I now knew was called the Plaza of the Centuries.

There was another small crowd around him; I recognized some of the same people – small, seedy *barraquistes* with an air of resignation to them, the resignation of the defeated. It was depressing – they had probably already taken The Treatment, since few people kept putting it off until they were in their thirties. And now they were doomed to an eternity of dreary resignation.

I didn't know what they heard in the violinist's music: the sound were random and raucous, high-pitched squeals, and unmusical screeches that pained the eardrum. But, as I approached, the disconnected sounds once again became compelling, moving with a current that was irresistible.

The mood suddenly fell apart, and the sounds of raucous sawing returned. The violinist was staring at me, his skullface expressionless behind those scarlet electroglasses, the bow still sawing away at the strings. He turned away from me abruptly and concentrated on the music once more. The sudden moment of disorientation was gone, and I was swept away, caught in a turbulence of melody.

Dreams and fantasies whipped through my head too quickly to catalog or even identify: stars and planets, shattered moons and nebulae, crystal forests, long jagged canyons of red rock, dust storms, emaciated elongated creatures living always on the verge of death, breathless rushing icy rivers filled with jagged rocks and ice floes, towering mountains where sheer cliffs plunged thousands of meters to razored rocks. It was a disorienting trip, and I was stunned and shaken when he reached the final, violent, discordant note.

There was a long moment of silence before the audience recovered enough to applaud. A surprisingly large crowd had gathered, much larger than the small handful that had been clustered around him when I had arrived. Feeling almost as if I were being pulled to him, I walked over.

"You were here yesterday, weren't you?" he said in a sepulchral whisper.

"Yes. I was."

"I thought so."

"My name's Sanchez Madeira." I held out my hand. "I'd like to talk to you."

"They call me Blind Joe Death, though I'm neither blind nor dead." His hand touched his electroglasses briefly. "And *I* would like to talk to *you*, Sanchez Madeira. Where shall we talk and what shall we talk about?"

"Are you going to play any more?" a small, beaten-looking man asked plaintively.

"That's all," Blind Joe Death said hoarsely. "I'm not playing any more today." He held a bony hand out to me in an oddly cavalier fashion. Swallowing my distaste, I took it briefly. It was dry yet slippery, like a fine plastic.

"You didn't have to be so rude to that guy," I said.

"If I kept playing whenever someone wanted me to," he said curtly, "I'd be playing all night long."

"Why do you come out here then? The way you play you could be working in a club instead of playing for nixies and millies."

"You think so? Have you heard me from the other side of the plaza?"

"Yes."

"Would *you* pay to hear someone play like that?"

"Well, no. But when I got closer..." I hesitated.

"Yes? What happened when you got closer?"

"The music... changed somehow; there were different touches to it."

"What kind of... touches?"

"It was more than just music. It was scenes, emotions, impressions."

"Let me tell you something, Sanchez Madeira." He motioned toward a bench and we sat down. "That crowd that you saw at the end, that was the largest crowd I've ever drawn. Those touches of mine, as you call them, ordinarily extend only a short distance, not even the width of this plaza. But today, something happened to change that. Do you know anything about violins?"

"I've known a couple of people who played one. And there was this guy who played classical music on one a couple of years ago, really famous..."

"Yes, yes, of course." His sepulchral whisper seemed to get stronger. "Mine is just an ordinary, unmodified violin, no different from the ancient instrument of centuries ago. The projections, as you call them, the emotional images, seem to come from me, yet they seem to be somehow connected to my violin-playing."

"Sounds like quite a violin," I said, more flippantly than I felt. To tell the truth, Blind Joe Death's grandiosity was getting on my nerves.

"There's nothing extraordinary about my violin." He focused his electroglass gaze on me – they conveyed no discernible emotion. "I'd never felt the projections myself until yesterday, although other people have told me about them. And I've never drawn anywhere near as many people as I did today. Someone else was projecting them back to me."

"And you think it was me?"

"It happened yesterday and it happened today, and you were here both times."

"There were a lot of other people here today. It could've been anyone."

"I don't think so."

Was he right? Was there something about me that amplified his projections to a larger audience? I've heard about all kinds of strange extra-sensory abilities but I had never heard of a human amplifier.

"We could be partners," he said in that hoarse whisper of his.

"Why would I want to be your partner? Cadging nixies and millies on street corners."

"You could end up doing that yourself someday, you know."

"Maybe. Maybe so. But that's no reason for doing it now."

He looked at me for a long moment. "All right, if that's the way you see it."

He started to leave and I felt a sudden panic: suppose he was right. There had to be some kind of way of making big money with this talent of his, and I was losing my chance to be a part of it.

"Wait a minute," I said, as casually as possible. "Exactly what did you have in mind?"

"Alone, neither of us is exactly a star. You're a club musician and I'm just a street beggar." I started to protest but he held up a cautionary hand. "There's no need to get upset by the truth, Sanchez Madeira. You're no longer young; therefore you haven't had the success you've dreamed of, and the chances get less and less each day. I don't think you've taken The Treatment, and I don't know why; but that's not my business."

"Okay, okay," I said in a low, tight voice. "Get on with it."

"As I said, neither of us has been much of a success separately. Between us, though, we could go a lot further than either of us could go alone. I don't know what it is that happens between us but we've both felt it and we know what it's like. People would pay for that, Madeira. We wouldn't be playing on street corners; we'd be playing in concert halls."

He had me. He had me like a sea-creature wriggling on a hook and he knew he had me, the bloody-eyed devil. I didn't like it but I had to play it out and find out if it would work, if it was the ticket I was looking for, the ticket that would take me out of my dreary club crawl. If it didn't work, I wouldn't be in any worse shape I already was in.

We worked for the next half-hour, making sure that it was some kind of interaction between the two of us, Blind Joe playing in one corner of the square while I moved around, trying to find the limits of his projections. The phenomenon ceased when I had left the square entirely, only to begin again as soon as I walked back.

$\wp \lessdot \gtrdot \wp$

My boots were covered with the mud of the unpaved streets by the time we reached his home.

Blind Joe lived in a ramshackle construction of stucco that apparently had once been a mosque in one of the filthiest sections of the *barraque*, the top layer of pale green paint flaking off revealed large splotches of the underlying pink. The windows and doorways were all arched, coming to points, with intricate scrollwork barely visible around them. Every window was boarded. Like most slums, this area had known better days.

The door opened to a large unfurnished room with small cubicles on either side. An old man sat in rags in front of one of the rooms, humming to himself. The large room smelled of dust and old urine.

Blind Joe's cubicle had a long mat against one wall and two cushions on the opposite wall. Two large candles provided the only illumination.

I checked the tuning on my autar. Blind Joe looked at me oddly for a moment then took out his violin. He asked me to start, then joined me after two bars. There was no magic, none of the images, just the scraping of bow against strings while I tried to follow him with the autar and the computer tried to follow me. It was a disaster.

"It's that instrument of yours," Blind Joe said. "I need something softer, something more subtle. Can you play a guitar?"

"Hell, no. the only instrument I know how to play is the autar."

"There's not much difference between an autar and a guitar," he said quietly.

"The hell there isn't!"

We argued for half an hour, me screaming while Blind Joe stated his arguments in that hoarse whisper of his. The fact that he wasn't yelling only made me scream even more. I finally agreed to try the guitar a friend of his was conveniently selling. It didn't turn out to be as difficult as I had expected. I tuned it to the top six strings of the autar and didn't have too much trouble, although I kept searching for the other strings. It wasn't Ski Barnstable, it wasn't Garcia, but once Blind Joe started to project, no one would know anyway.

❧ ◆ ❧

I was in a foul mood when I got to the club that night. The dream had become a nightmare. Blind Joe was running things and I didn't like taking orders from him – I cherished my freedom too much. The dreams of million-plat recording contracts, those lovely lights spelling out my name, and The Treatment, still glowed, but their edges were badly tarnished.

I looked at the stranger in the holomirror – already I could see crows' feet beginning to form around my eyes. My red hair was dark and dull – although I didn't see any gray hairs, I wouldn't have been surprised to find one – it was only a matter of time. The incipient jowls and hanging flesh of old age were all too obvious to me. I tried to grin at the stranger, but she just grimaced back at me. I took a gulp of the purple joe I had taken into the back room and it burned all the way down.

My performances that night were the worst sets I'd done yet at the Offnote.

The next morning, before going to see Blind Joe Death again, I went to one of the public terminals. It took a little searching, and a fair amount of money, but I finally found the information I was looking for, about the concert violinist of a few years back. His name was Zarias D'Nolfand. He had been an upcoming young soloist, with an eye for the ladies. There were a couple of holos, and he had been quite good-looking, a real matinee idol, with a classic sharp profile with a noble Roman nose, lips that were a little on the thin side but not too much so, and deep soulful eyes. His carefully trimmed hair was just a little bit tousled. The transformation from Zarias D'Nolfand to Blind Joe Death was about as complete as it could have been.

It was those good looks that had been his undoing. One of his paramours had decided that, if she couldn't have him all to herself, then no one would have him. One morning, when he was sleeping peacefully in her bed, she had poured acid all over him. By the time his screams had brought the neighbors, the police, and the emergency crews, much of his skin was gone, as well as his eyes and part of his larynx. They reached him before any serious damage was done to any of his internal organs, except for his lungs, and he survived, in a manner of speaking.

So, when I waded through the streets of the *barraque* to Blind Joe Death's mosque, I had a few cards in *my* hand.

"You're late," he said.

"Hey, man, I'm only human, you know? I had to perform last night, and I do need to sleep occasionally."

"I suppose that means you didn't practice any?"

"Not a lick, Zarias." He twitched quite noticeably at that. "No use denying it. I obviously hit a nerve."

"How did you find out?" His voice seemed even hoarser than usual.

"Just did a little research this morning. I figured it might help if I knew something about my partner."

"All right, you know. Let's rehearse."

I took out the guitar and began to tune it laboriously, cursing Blind Joe Death for insisting I use an instrument that needed to be tuned manually. "Look, let me ask you something." I took his silence for acquiescence. "You had lots of money a couple of years ago. You still do, don't you?" No response. "You don't have to do this garbage; you could just stay in your own little hideaway or, for that matter, get yourself fixed properly."

"Do you know what I'd look like? Nothing like what I was before. Not at all." There was a note of pride in his voice.

"You *like* looking the way you do now?"

"People notice me. I'm Blind Joe Death, not just another streetbeggar, not just one of the groundlings. I may not be Zaraias D'Nolfand anymore but I'm still somebody. I should think *you* would be able to understand that, Madeira." I did.

"There was no way they could have restored my face or body to what it had been before; there wasn't enough of a base to anchor anything to. They couldn't do much better than this. And even that little bit would cost, Madeira, it would cost, without any guarantees, without much hope at all."

"What about your friends?"

"Friends? What friends? Oh, they all came to the hospital in the beginning but, as soon as it was obvious I had nothing for them anymore, that I'd never get back on the concert stage again, they all drifted quickly off."

"All of them?"

"Every single last son of a bitch."

I shivered. I could see the same thing happening to me, except that I didn't really have any friends in the first place. Traveling from place to place, all by myself, I never got close to anyone.

Blind Joe was impervious to any more questioning, so we spent the rest of the time putting our act together, preparing for our unsuspected debut at the Offnote.

That came two days later. I went onstage alone first, carrying both the guitar and my autar. I began with my usual opening instrumental on autar, nervous and scared but also high and excited. My hands were covered with oily sweat and I dropped a few notes. I did two more songs, then saw Blind Joe in the shadows off to the side of the Offnote's tiny stage. I finished my song and waited for the smattering of polite applause to die down.

"I'd like to introduce my partner for the next few songs. Mr. Blind Joe Death."

At the sight of Blind Joe, the audience became restive and uneasy. There was a faint sheen on his bone-white skin. I picked up the guitar and looked at him; he nodded, and I began a simple run, slow and dreamy, one note at a time. In the middle of the second bar, Blind Joe began a low quavery note. I was seized by a sudden panic; would it work now, when it counted most? I didn't know how to control the projections, and I didn't think Blind Joe did, either.

In my panic, I almost wished the planet could swallow me and hide me. I could feel it yawning open slowly underneath me, and I felt myself, falling, falling, growing hotter and hotter as the innards of Clayton's Peacock pulsed redly around me. I landed in the middle of a river of lava, pulled along roughly by the current, swallowing molten mineral, my whole body being consumed in inside and out, by the flame, the burning, the torment. The lava river ended in a volcano that erupted sending me spinning slowly into the depths of space, now burnt and seared by the absolute cold of vacuum. I held my hand in front of me. I could see the bones beneath the skin, the stars and Clayton's sun shining through the tracery of veins. My lungs ached, yearning for air, for breath. I landed on a barren rock, spinning emptily through the void, where an eternity passed in loneliness. I cried a million tears. I felt an agony and an ache in my breast that I thought would never end.

Then it ended. I was alone on a tiny stage on a minor planet at the edge of the galaxy. There was a long, long silence, then someone started to applaud hesitantly. It was slowly picked up, just as hesitantly and uncertainly, until everyone in the entire room was standing unsteadily on their feet.

Beside me, a hoarse voice said, "Thank you." Blind Joe bowed slightly, as if he were in formal attire, his arms stiffly at his sides, the violin and bow in his hands.

He motioned me to begin our next number, and we sent the audience hurtling down precipitous slopes; we forced them to experience tragic love affairs; we met them in blind alleys and beat them to a pulp; we distributed their constituent atoms and molecules to the stellar winds. They felt stars dying, asteroids in agony, moons on collision courses. When Blind Joe and I were done, the audience was shaken and pale. We were none too steady ourselves, but we were high as well, high and flying.

When we left the Offnote, a small group of people was waiting for us, fidgeting a little, shifting from foot to foot.

"What do you want?" Blind Joe asked hoarsely.

"Are you going to perform here again?" one of them asked softly.

"Yeah," I said, still excited. "We just signed a new contract."

"But we're only going to do one show a night," Blind Joe said.

"Thank you." They backed off as Blind Joe walked forward, apparently afraid of being touched by him. I thought I heard him chuckle.

ॐ ◀ ▶ ॐ

The Offnote was jammed on the following night, which delighted me. "Just look at all those people," I said to Joe. "They haven't even heard us yet, probably never heard *of* us until this morning."

"Groundlings." Blind Joe made it into a swear word. "They live their sheltered little lives, trying to get their danger safely. That's all they want from us. They want to eat us alive."

There were quite a few small-time promoters in that second night's crowd. They clustered around us after our performance, making us all kinds of lucrative-sounding offers.

Blind Joe waited while they all clamored for his attention. When they had finally talked themselves out, he said, "Have any of you got anything in writing?" The clamor died down abruptly. "When you've got something solid to offer us, come see me. Until then, don't waste your breath and my time." He walked away, through his silent phalanx of admirers, into the Clayton's Peacock night of scanty stars.

Even though I knew he was right, I was ticked off by his arrogance. All right, he had been at the top and he knew the pitfalls to watch out for. Nonetheless, it pissed me off that he hadn't bothered to even ask for my opinion.

"Why haven't you taken The Treatment?" he asked me curtly half an hour before our performance the following night.

"Why do you want to know?" I asked suspiciously.

"Just curious. You know about me. Maybe I'd like to know something about you. Well?"

"I was waiting," I said cautiously.

"Waiting? Waiting for what? For the universe to implode?"

"No," I said sharply. "I just... I just didn't want to go into debt."

"What difference does it make? No one cares how much money you owe anymore."

"I care. I like my freedom." Blind Joe gave a disparaging snort. "What about you? Have you taken The Treatment?"

"Yes." His voice was barely audible.

"So you've got to live forever looking like that?"

"Not forever." His voice was now an intense whisper. "Someday they'll be able to make me look the way I used to. Till then..." He stopped.

"It may be a long time."

"I can wait."

A long time. And I would be a long time paying off The Treatment unless my partnership with Blind Joe Death worked. I could understand why someone would put off the Treatment until the last moment, trying desperately to avoid those bonds, but I couldn't understand why anyone would totally refuse it. But Garcia had refused, and Wainer, and others: Ipnasele, who had developed and perfected the percussive effects of the autar; Lal Behari Day, SwetBestanta, Pantschatantra, and the inescapable, unavoidable Sir Degarre, whose music could not be ignored.

Degarre had committed suicide only forty years after taking The Treatment; his later music had never quite reached the power, strength, and energy of his earlier work.

They were giants and I couldn't quite understand them. I could never understand why or how they could possibly refuse The Treatment.

⤝⟨⟩⤞

Two promoters came backstage that night with non-conflicting offers Blind Joe read and promptly agreed to. When he gave me the contracts for my print, I hesitated.

"There's no need for you to read them," Blind Joe said crossly. "Even though they're not great offers, they're not bad. We can't expect anything better right now."

"I'd like to make my own decisions, if you don't mind." His imperious manner irritated me.

"Don't you trust me?"

"It's not a matter of trust. We're supposed to be partners and I'd like to have a hand in the decisions, if you don't mind."

One of the promoters stepped in. "It's a little early for you two to be fighting, isn't it? You've just started working together. Why don't you keep the contracts overnight and study them?"

I eagerly agreed while Blind Joe grumbled his assent. As soon as we were alone, he said, "What are you trying to do? Make me look bad?"

"Me make *you* look bad? If you want me as your partner, Joe, you're going to have to treat me as one, not just some little slave to do whatever you say."

"I've been in this business longer than you have, Madeira, and I've been to the top."

"Sure, okay. But that's no reason for you to go making decisions for both us. I'm not a child, and I'm not going to let you treat me like one. We've got enough time to go over things in private."

"All right," Blind Joe grumbled. "Let's go over these contracts and I'll show you why we should accept them."

Our first concert was in Buckdancer, a small city several hundred klicks away. I was surprised when several of our little coterie of followers at the Offnote showed up. I was even more surprised when I saw the face of one of them in the front holo of a newscopy. I keyed the story:

"Gabael Paviotso, a resident of Brokedown Palace, was discovered drowned in the Apparition River this morning. Friends of his, who had come with Paviotso to Buckdancer to attend a concert last night, said he had been depressed recently, but the news of his death came as a surprise. There was no evidence of foul play, and authorities say they consider Paviotso's death to be either a suicide or a tragic accident. His friends had last seen Paviotso..."

I keyed the story off as a chilly snake of apprehension crawled around my chest. I went to Blind Joe's to play the story for him.

"So what?" he asked.

"What do you mean, so what?"

"Why did you bring that story to me? Why should I care what happens to some fool who doesn't have enough sense to take care of himself?"

"He committed *suicide*."

"All right then, suicide, accident, carelessness, it's all the same. He didn't have enough sense to take care of himself."

"But he was one of our fans," I insisted.

"What do you want me to do? Hold his hand, watch him every second? Watch every one of them? Be serious, Madeira."

I was convinced we were somehow responsible for Paviotso's death, even if I couldn't bring myself to say that outright to Blind Joe, not wanting to face his laughter and derision. Our performances were filled with images of death and danger, depressing even when exciting. I was certain anyone who experienced several of them would be affected. I wondered if I myself had been affected, although I didn't feel any different.

We took off like a rocket, quickly becoming the hottest act on Clayton's Peacock. It seemed to me that after every concert there would be one or two deaths among our growing body of followers. I kept expecting the police to arrest us or something. But apparently I was the only one who noticed the coincidences, if indeed that was all they were. But I was sure they weren't. After each performance, there would be a large crowd of them outside the stage door, oddly silent – *deathly* silent, I kept thinking – and they parted to let Blind Joe pass, not attempting to touch either of us or prevent our passage. It was eerie, to say the least.

I confronted Blind Joe about the multiple deaths among our followers, but he still wasn't concerned. "I don't care if we *are* responsible," he said. "They're old enough to take care of themselves. I won't take the blame. If they can't handle it, it's their problem, not mine."

We were offered a contract to perform as the second act in a large concert at the capitol city, but Blind Joe refused it. When I asked him why he didn't want to do it, he said, "Look at that auditorium. It's too large. We can't handle an audience of that size."

"Are you sure?"

"Not entirely. But I'd hate to find out the hard way that I'm right. All I know is that's a bigger crowd than any we've handled yet. Before we take on an auditorium that size, we've got to find out how large an area my ability affects."

"*Your* ability? If it wasn't for me..."

"Furthermore," he continued, ignoring my outburst, "I've had an offer from another promoter." He grinned his death's-head grin. "He's offering us a solo concert the same day."

"Where?"

"At another auditorium in the capital."

"What? That's not fair, Joe. We'll draw people from the other concert." The idea just didn't seem right to me. We performers needed to hang together, not compete with each other unnecessarily.

I could swear that his grin grew wider. "Yes, I suppose we will. With our reputation, we'll probably draw quite a few people away from that concert."

"But that's just not fair," I repeated.

"Fair? I don't know anything about fair." His hoarse whisper grew even hoarser as it increased in intensity. "Was it fair when someone threw acid in my face? Was it fair when my agent, and everybody else, turned their backs on me? Don't talk to me about fairness, Madeira."

"But..."

"All I know, Madeira, is that we're getting a big guarantee out of this. If some promoter loses his shirt, that's his problem."

"What about the other performers? Won't we be taking their audience away from them?"

"Madeira, when are you going to stop worrying about other people and start looking out for yourself?"

He stalked out of the room, leaving me alone with my thoughts. His statement about "his" ability still rankled – I had become nothing a tool to him, a human amplifier, not even as important as his violin. No matter what I wanted, no matter what I said, we always wound up doing things his way – I played the guitar instead of the autar because *he* wanted me to, and now we would do a concert that would split the audience and cause bad feelings simply because he wanted some kind of revenge.

When *was* I going to look out for myself? When would I stop letting him lead me around by the nose? I had been free before, but now I was just an appendage to Blind Joe Death. We had finally reached the point where the big money would be coming in, and soon I would be able to take The Treatment without fear of being in debt for very long. But was it worth it? I had already lost my freedom. A part of me was dying under him. I was afraid I would lose my own free will and never be able to regain it if I stayed with him any longer.

I had to break free. I hadn't written any new songs since we had met, and there seemed to be nothing left inside me to write.

I looked at my face in the holomirror. I saw the skull beneath the skin, and the worm beneath the skull. I thought of Garcia and of Wainer; I thought of Ipnasele and Sir Degarre. And I thought of Gabael Piviotso. I thought of The Treatment, and something within me seemed to die. Something within me always, always had been dying, and always would be dying. Until I took The Treatment. Then there would be nothing left to die. Like Paviotso and Blind Joe Death, I would be dead inside. There would be no more songs to write. And I finally understood what Garcia had meant: Without death, there would be no songs, no art, nothing but fear and timidity.

I saw my face forever young. And I saw Blind Joe Death. I saw his callousness become mine; I saw my despair become his bitterness. And it made me angry. For a moment, the clean, bright anger burned, then it was replaced by determination, a fierce determination stronger than any I'd ever known before. Then by a smile, a smile that threatened to become a triumphant laugh that didn't quite break through.

I went back to the instruments, cradling the guitar for a long moment, surprised my cheeks were wet. In the time I had been with Blind Joe, I had learned to love and respect the instrument. But it didn't belong to me; it was Blind Joe Death's. I put it in its case then picked up my autar case, leaving the guitar behind.

I stopped in the doorway, indecisive. "The son of a bitch owes me that much," I said to no one. I went back, picked up the guitar, and left, heading back to the streets and the clubs were I belonged. Maybe I wouldn't live forever, but at least I'd *live* and just maybe I'd create something that would last longer than me.

For some reason, the triumphant smile wouldn't leave my face.

The End

AFTERWORD
BY GRANT CARRINGTON

It has been interesting preparing these pieces for e-publication. Since they were written on a typewriter 30-40 years ago and published before I owned my first computer (an Apple IIe), I have had to enter them into my computer prior to publication. There have been times when I have cringed at the clumsy prose of my so-much younger self but there have also been times when I have been amazed at "my" lyricism. I guess that sounds pretty conceited, but I feel as if I am looking at the writing of another man, a man who is writing in a way that I no longer can and wish I could, not just because it was the way I wrote, but also because it was the way I experienced and lived (or tried to). I have to smile at that 35-year-old boy who felt he was so old but still felt with an intensity and energy that seems to be no longer possible for me. But it sure feels good to re-experience it, if only second-hand.

On the other hand, some of that "lyricism" turned into purple prose, which I found hard to stomach but had to leave in place because fixing it would be making too large a change in the original stories.

In entering these stories into computer format, it was inevitable that I would do some editing, but I have tried to keep the changes minor. A lot of commas and unnecessary "he/she said"s were deleted and a few commas added. A handful of sentences were so painful to my current sensibilities that I had to recast them, notably the very first sentence of *Time's Fool*, which had been "Waves of conversation crested on Garcia's ears, like the somnolent disharmonies of Vlatko's

'Modular' Symphony, as the autarist moved through the party" in the Doubleday printing. All the words are still there, just in a different order. Many times I had to just grit my teeth and accept them as that alien young man had written them--it wouldn't have meant just one sentence but rewriting an entire section.

One of the most embarrassing parts is the inverted syntax of Bwire and other characters. It is made even worse that it is similar to that of Yoda in *Star Wars*. But "Stella Blue" was published 3 years before the first *Star Wars* movie was released. (Now the truth can be told: I am a secret timedipper who came back from 1977 to 1974 so I could use Yoda's inverted syntax in my own stories.)

And Garcia's distant-future world seems to me to be remarkably similar to that of 1974. I didn't do a very good job of predicting the future--all the computers are wired into a mainframe similar to those found in governments and corporations in 1974. At least I did call it a personal computer, even though PC's were still about 10 years in the future and mine was hardwired to a main frame. (Though I'm probably not the first sf writer to use that terminology before personal computers were invented.) As for the internet, well, it was barely a gleam in DARPANet's eye in 1974. And as for the telephone (or holostage), in 1974 we were all still wired to the phone company and, if you weren't home, well, you just had to drop a quarter in one of those pay-phone shells that already had replaced most of Gotham's phone booths. Cell phones didn't exist and, I blush to admit, they or something similar do not seem to exist anywhere in the universe of *Time's Fool*. Mea culpa; mea maxima culpa.

If you were one of the few who used a credit card, it was put in one of those credit card impression doo-hickeys and you were given a carbon copy while the original was sent off to the credit card company via... the United States Post Office.

The manned space program had come to a halt and the space shuttle program was still in its infancy.

It all began with "Annapolis Town." And "Annapolis Town" began when Robin Scott Wilson, founder of the Clarion SF&F Workshop, told me, "I wish your stories had as much emotion in them as your songs do." So I went home and wrote the story, which shares its title with that of one of my songs. Other than that, they both take place in Annapolis and are about love and love lost, and that's about all they have in common.

"Stella Blue" takes its title from the Grateful Dead song of the same name but I have absolutely no idea any more of what prompted the story itself.

"What Are You Going to Do When You See Your Lady Strolling on the Deck of the Starship?" is the title of a song on the first Jefferson Starship album, *Blows Against the Empire*. Once again, I no longer have no idea where the story came from, although it is enhanced (I hope) from my experiences as a light crew techie.

"The Worm Beneath the Skull" was inspired by the cover for the Grateful Dead album, *Blues For Allah*. I no longer remember how it got from that inspiration to this particular story. Although there's no time travel in it, there are references to Garcia (of *Time's Fool*) and Michael Shaara's "Wainer," which I consider the finest sf story I've ever read.

Which brings me finally to *Time's Fool* itself. Perhaps it was triggered by an article in *Scientific American* about the thymus gland. In any case, I was already at work on it when I told Pat LoBrutto, then an editor at Doubleday, about it and soon I had a contract to finish the damn thing. Its original title had been *The Edge of the Wine*, resulting in a number of references to wine, apparently wherever I could fit them in, before I had retitled it.

I found as I read it that I wanted to make major changes and some of my mannerisms annoyed the hell out of me. Since I don't smoke, my characters have a tendency to nod their heads or smile far too often. I got rid of the ones that served no purpose but there are still far too many. And I sure was having a love affair (and still am) with ellipses. (That's probably because of my math background.) Hopefully the average reader, whoever or whatever he or she may be, will not notice them as much as this jaded author.

This was the first time I have read the whole thing through since it had been published in 1981 and, while much of it is painful for me to read, there are sections that amaze me. How did that 40-year-old me do it? I certainly can't write like that today. As Richard Rodgers said (via Yul Brynner in *The King and I*), "Is a puzzlement."

When you look at the differences between America and the rest of the world between 1900 and 2000, the differences between 1980 and whenever this takes place seem very minimal. Already, in 2013, we have surpassed many of the descriptions in this novel and we aren't that far from leaving the rest of this so-called "future society" in our dust.

Then there's immortality. The use of the thymus gland was consistent with theory at the time, as far as I could tell. In fact, as far as I know, it still is, though the use of radiation to modify the tissues is pure fantasy. Today, though, we're looking at telomeres and low calorie diets and nanotechnology.

At the very end of the book, there are words that spoke to me today in a surprising way, a way that probably will not touch many other readers, but their effect on me is so strong, I have to mention them. "In the silence Garcia could hear the sounds of sirens and of distant amplified voices, the faint echo of shouts of rage, of tiny cheers." This brought back memories of the demonstrations of the Sixties, of standing on the steps of the administration building looking down at the crowd below us, wondering how I had gotten up there and really wanting to be down in the crowd.

"He was *alive*, come what may, come death and extinction, as surely it must. You can't go back, he thought, and you can't stand still. He had to go forward or he would surely die. That was where his strength and his art lay, in the constant fight against Death, spitting in its very face, not in conquering it and then living in a fearful immortality. So he would die. So what?" I was 40 years old, halfway between the crib and the grave, just beginning to come to grips with my own mortality. Now the grave is within sight and the crib is long gone and those words seem more real and true to me now than they probably did then. Thank you, 40-year-old Grant Carrington, and thank you, Deb Houdek Rule, for allowing me to reread them after all these years.

After 32 years, does it hold up? There are large sections that I would like to take a sledgehammer to and rewrite from scratch but there also many places I wouldn't dare change a word of, for fear the whole thing would fall apart like a house of cards, and I know, that if I were to write it today, it would be a very different story. But the characters would remain the same. So, as usual, I guess it's up to you, the reader, to decide if it still has any merit.

Grant Carrington

www.ingramcontent.com/pod-product-compliance
Lightning Source LLC
Chambersburg PA
CBHW020313200626
46814CB00006BA/2231